For my wonderful grandson, Finlay

Dead Ed in my Head
by Barbara Catchpole

Published by Raven Books
An imprint of Ransom Publishing Ltd.
Unit 7, Brocklands Farm, West Meon, Hampshire GU32 1JN, UK
www.ransom.co.uk

ISBN   978 178591 633 5
First published in 2017

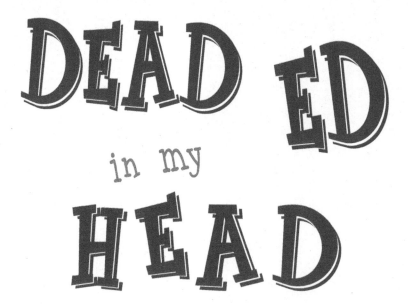

BARBARA CATCHPOLE

RAVEN

*In which Tod shouts a lot, gets thrown
out of class and signs a contract.*

'Why don't you just **** off!'

The kids gasped. Some grinned, but most just waited, pleased for a bit of excitement. This was better than fractions!

A large number of the kids put their pens down, leaned back in their chairs and mentally encouraged the boy: *Go for it, this is brilliant!* The ginger boy next to Tod, who still hadn't found his Maths book, stopped ferreting about in his bag. A grin lit up his ferrety, freckly face. His ferrety front teeth were on display.

Some kids turned towards Tod, their mouths hanging open like particularly dim goldfish.

Tod stood up, shouting full-pelt at the teacher. He felt the blood pounding in his ears and he clenched his fists in anger. There were spots in front of his eyes and he felt that little vein throb above his left eyebrow. The shouting felt very good.

He was a good six inches taller than Mr Jones and, as he moved towards him, the guy backed off, making little flapping motions with his hands, his eyes darting about looking for an escape.

At that moment Tod felt pure hatred.

He hated the man's stupid cartoon tie and matching socks.

He hated his stupid comb-over.

He hated his stupid brown jacket with its patches on the elbows. (What was that about? W*****!)

He hated the flappy little movements he was making with his hands.

He hated his bad breath and the way he laughed at his own weak little jokes.

He hated his half-human, half-goldfish classmates, especially the extremely fit Bianca Clark whose silly, fit, lip-glossed lips made a little glistening, strawberry O of excitement. She looked like the stupid one-eyed alien on 'Futurama'. Except with two eyes.

He hated the world and some of the closer planets.

'I don't care what you think! I don't care! You don't know my parents!'

Not so big now, are you? Not so adult and sarcastic? Not so mature! Do you think I might hit you? Well I actually might. I might strangle you with your sad Mickey Mouse tie and stuff the matching socks in your mouth. I would like to, oh yes, I would like to hit you hard. Right on your particularly ugly, squashy, red road-map nose.

OK, so Tod *had* been daydreaming in Maths. He'd had

English before Maths and they'd done a poem by Seamus Heaney. It was something about Heaney's father. How his father had been, like, this huge guy who took him out on the farm, ploughing with big old farm horses, and how he admired him.

Tod had listened to his English teacher read it and had been there himself – in a world where you were little and the big people took care of you. He was out of the classroom and into the open air, ploughing the field and his dad was his hero, sailing the plough like a huge sailing ship.

Tod remembered how he had felt about his own father before The Affair with That Slapper. Admittedly his father didn't have a team of farm horses – there wasn't much call for that round Tod's way (there wasn't even much of a back garden) – but his dad could bowl 175 on a good day.

Tod had loved bowling with him, every Friday night. He'd loved the smell of the bowling alley and the excitement of getting a strike. He loved the wait while the pins toppled over into each other and the noise they made. He had even loved sitting on the plastic chairs in the café eating greasy chips.

His dad had really listened to him on a Friday night. Tod had been able to talk to him, ask advice or tell him about school. His dad obviously hadn't shared his own thoughts and feelings, though, as he'd run away with That Woman Who Wears Her Skirts Up To Her Bum without telling Tod 'The Plan'.

He had betrayed Tod.

Then Tod got to thinking how it was written 'Seamus' but pronounced 'Shay-mus', and he thought about the new girl who everyone had called 'Sy – ob – han' for a whole day, like an alien when her name 'Siobhan' was apparently pronounced 'Shiv - orn'.

What was that about? What *were* her parents thinking? She must have had to explain that like a zillion times. Thank goodness his name was easy! You couldn't really mess up 'Tod'. It meant 'death' in German though, which wasn't so nice. If he went to Germany, he would be really cool. He could wear black all the time and watch people's eyes as he introduced himself.

'My name is Death. Na – ha-ha-ha!'

He hoped the new baby would be given a decent name. Not Tracey or Martin, *puh-lease*. He would have to have a word with Mum …

CRACK!

The teacher had brought the board rubber down on Tod's desk, making him jump, and then had started on at him for not listening.

Tod had just waited – Mr Jones would run out of steam eventually. But there was no real need for the board rubber thing, was there? Really? He could have just pointed out nicely that he would have liked Tod's attention. It was a bit rude.

That's when Tod had started to feel angry – a little fire had started in the pit of his stomach.

Mr Jones had also been enjoying *his* good shout though.

His old Ford Fiesta needed a four-hundred-pound repair.

His wife's mother was coming for the weekend. He hated her – *and* she watched 'Coronation Street'.

The head of department wanted to watch his lesson later, 'to make supportive suggestions' and 'to encourage good practice' – which meant telling him he was a rubbish teacher again.

His piles were playing up again and this boy – this horrible, hairy boy – was sitting in his lesson, drawing. What was it? It looked like a bowling ball he was drawing in the margin of his book. This particular irritating shaggy-haired boy – and several others – had to get a C grade for Mr Jones to meet his all-important ('you won't get a pay rise') target – and the boy had all the mathematical talent of a gerbil. A young, hairy, brainless and probably vicious little gerbil, too. Not even your average gerbil. The sort that your mum bought you for Christmas and it bit your thumb during the Queen's Speech.

'Your parents can't have brought you up very well if you don't value the education provided for you! Do you want to be stupid all your life? How immature!'

Mr Jones was really worked up now and little flecks of spittle flew from his mouth onto Tod and Tod's book. That was when Tod started shouting. He hadn't really made a conscious decision to shout. It was funny – one moment he was sitting being spat on and the next minute he was shouting. It was like he went from 0 to 60 miles an hour in sixty seconds.

'Get out of this classroom! You will *not* use language like that to a member of staff!'

Well, I just have – obviously! Tod took several deep breaths like his mentor had told him, and almost immediately felt regret for his outburst (and slightly dizzy). He still felt sick and angry though, and he was still swimming in a deep pool of hatred and resentment.

He did his best to spoil the drama of the teacher's moment.

He made sure he took ages to get his books together.

He upset his chair.

He apologised nicely, interrupting the bloke going on about fractions.

He left.

He knocked on the door and went back in to look for his pen, coughing a lot on the way, apologising again ('Sorr-ee!').

In fact, he tried really hard to be downright irritating. His blood still pounded in his ears and the little dots still blurred his vision. He would leave when he was ready to leave.

He left because he thought Mr Jones might actually have a fit. The man was almost purple with suppressed rage and the little hairs actually seemed to be sticking out of his ears at right angles.

Tod then spent about a quarter of an hour amusing the class by staring back in through the classroom window. Bianca gave him a little wave and made a kissy face.

Then a big hand fell on his shoulder. The Behaviour Patrol bloke had caught him.

An hour later, he sat outside the Learning Mentor's office looking at the water stain on the wall that looked like a kangaroo upside-down.

The whole school had moved into in a brand-new building, but some sort of peculiar process was happening and the new building was changing back into the old building. It was like magic. You could really see it happening.

There was a lot of vandalism. The door handles came unscrewed really easily. Already there was chewing gum in many of the electricity sockets and under the handrails. The site maintenance guy was developing a hernia keeping the white walls free of graffiti. He would paint over it on Friday and it would all be back by Monday break. It was just too easy!

For some reason all the corridor lights were on chains

hanging from the ceiling, so the bigger boys could easily jump up and bat them as they walked along.

The biggest design point was the open walkway above the canteen, from which you could throw things or even spit onto the heads of the lucky diners. Tod didn't do that because he felt it was gross. But he had on a number of occasions wondered if the blokes who built the academy were mentally deficient.

Tod found the decay of the new building comforting. He didn't like things to be too clean or organised. The other day he'd found a pizza in his room that had been there for at least three weeks. It had made a lovely smell – all cheesy and musty, and it had rather interesting furry bits. He expected his mum would throw it out after the baby was born, but at the moment she couldn't see the floor. She couldn't even see her own feet. She certainly couldn't reach it without a load of bother and a forklift.

Tod liked his room a lot. You could get in there and shut out everybody else in the world. He spent a great deal of his time just lying on his bed, staring at the ceiling and trying to think of nothing at all. Nearly all the things he liked doing were things you did alone. He contemplated the kangaroo water sign.

Kangaroos, Tod thought. *It would be cool to be a kangaroo.* They can really move, those guys. If anything upset you, you could run and run, just run across the bush until you felt better. Those huge back legs would just kick in and there was so much space in Australia. You could run for miles and miles without hitting a fence – *and* it was always sunny.

Kangaroos could hold things in their dinky little hands. And they were intelligent. There was a rerun of Skippy where Skippy had known that a kid had fallen down the mineshaft, even though

11

all the adults were just running about, shouting the kid's name and crying. No messing with having babies either; tiny little things like worms they are. They just climb up the mother and pop themselves into her pouch. Bet she doesn't even know she's had a baby. She would be just boing-ing along one day, put her dinky little hand down into her pouch for a kangaroo hanky or something and, 'Whoa ... how did that get there? I must have had a baby – must boing down to the post office and claim the child benefit.' Not like Mum, who is the size of a small bungalow.

I wonder how kangaroos have sex? Do they stop still? Do they bounce at the same time? She could keep condoms in her pocket! Not at the same time as her little wormy baby though. That would send a terrible message to the youngster.

'What are you thinking about, Tod?'

Mentor alert! Take cover! Prepare to be asked painfully embarrassing questions! Should he say, 'Kangaroos having sex'? Should he say, 'Condoms'? No! Panic!

'Nothing.'

'Come in and sit down, honey.'

And there she sat, looking at him, a painfully thin woman in a cardigan that looked like it had been put together in a car factory. Probably by robots. Blind robots. Wearing driving gloves. Or mittens. Furry mittens.

That really was an ugly woolly. It appeared to have little paper dolls holding hands embroidered around the bottom. (The bottom of the cardigan that was, not her bottom.) The cardigan's bottom was about twenty centimetres below hers.

Now he was thinking about her bottom! Couldn't he get a grip? Of his mind, not her bottom ...

Perhaps he was going mad. Was she sure it was a cardigan? It didn't really look comfortable as a cardigan, although Tod couldn't see another part of her body it would fit.

She wanted to understand him, he could see that. He could almost *feel* it. She loved teenagers and she really thought that if they were properly understood, there would be no problem.

Tod's mum didn't understand him, and he didn't even understand himself, so was she really in with a chance? He supposed she had been properly trained.

They were always having training days, the teachers. Tod found that a bit worrying. Most of his teachers were really old – over thirty at least. Why did they need so many training days just to say, 'Do the sums on page 39 – miss out exercise C – underline the date. Stop talking at the back!'?

Were they slow learners or what?

The mentor smiled at him, her pale blue eyes all watery behind enormous specs.

'What's the matter, sweetie? Do you have any problems? Any issues?'

'Tissues?'

'Issues!'

Issues, Tod thought. *Well, yes. My dad's left home with Lisa from Accounts. My mum says her skirt shows her bum. (Lisa's, that is.) He took my iPod. With absolutely superb timing, after fifteen years of either being very careful, no sex life or some sort of problem, he's left Mum pregnant. At the moment she is the size of a four-wheel-drive truck and keeps crying all the time.*

She keeps sending me down the road to the chemist for pile creams and stuff for after the birth. I'm only fifteen and I'm a boy; I'm not supposed to be able to talk to chemists. I'm supposed to just snatch stuff off the shelf and smuggle it to the counter or even straight out the door under my hoodie. The girl behind the counter makes it plain she thinks I've got a terminal disease, or perhaps she thinks I really fancy her, because she keeps saying, 'You again?' and giving me a really goofy grin. Then everybody looks at me.

Mum hasn't got anyone to be with her at the birth. I'm certainly not going to be there. If she asks, I'll have to emigrate. I might go to Australia and study kangaroos, because I'm interested in them. I can't cook, I can't wash, I can't iron and I can't deal with body parts.

'Er, nothing, nope,' said Tod.

'Sure?'

'Nope. Zip. I'm good.'

She stared at him for a bit and understood him a bit. She asked if he felt very sad and she carefully checked him out for suicidal tendencies.

He said he was hungry.

Then she took him down a floor to sit outside the Assistant Head of Year's office. Tod looked at a poster about the dangers of chlamydia.

Chlamydia – that would be a pretty name for a girl.

Tod read the poster.

Ooops! Perhaps not.

Whenever Tod read health information, he was sure he had the disease. He was now positive he had chlamydia, despite the fact that he had never even had a girlfriend. Not even held hands. Well, unless you counted Patti Snelson in Year 7, and she had just got stuck to him when they'd glued that Tudor Castle together.

It was perfectly normal not to have had sex at his age, Tod

14

reminded himself. At his age it was normal to be waiting. It was normal. Yes that was what he was doing – *waiting*.

Not that anyone had offered to have sex with him. It might be a long wait, but one would come along sooner or later – like the bus, but a lot more exciting, he hoped.

The teacher who had done the sex education lessons had said sixty per cent of sixteen-year-olds hadn't had sex. The boys had all sat there trying to look like the forty per cent and the girls had yawned as if they were too cool even to be in the class: too cool for school.

Tod suspected they *were*, actually, far too cool. They were like cats, girls. They did what they wanted when they wanted. They didn't need you. Get too near and you were scratched. Some of them terrified him – like Jade and Jodie in Year 11.

Jade and Jodie, queens of Year 11, stood on the top landing, looking down into the main open space of the Academy.

Jade was a very pretty mixed-heritage girl, white and Afro-Caribbean, her father a primary school teacher, her mother a nurse. Jade, as bright as a button, top sets for everything.

Jodie was clever as well, but not so fortunate: single mother, council estate, a little bit angry, a little bit scared, waiting for better times.

Jade admired the little tropical palm trees painted on her long white nails, holding her hand out in front of her as if the varnish was still drying. Both girls wore shed-loads of make up. They could get away with a lot as long as they stuck to natural colours.

As Jade explained patiently, 'They know we ain't got purple

eyelids or blue eyelashes. They ain't *stupid*. They know we don't *sparkle*.'

Their eyelashes were heavy, sweeping curtains, fake stuck in amongst the natural, held there by a heavy coating of black mascara. Like Japanese geishas they wore painted masks of foundation, which gathered in the few creases of their smooth, hopeful young faces and the folds of their tiny necks.

Their uniforms were as tight and skimpy as, again, they could get away with, and their ties were casually hanging down, the huge knot about two buttons down on the collar button.

Their big black school bags were in their lockers, to be collected after the last-minute trip to the toilets.

During break they clutched tiny sparkly little pink handbags, each containing make-up and a collapsible brush. Clompy high heels thudded as they walked.

When they did walk, it seemed the balcony might shake, like in Jurassic Park. Like tiny dinosaurs, the smaller kids parted to let them through. This was their queendom. They ruled the balcony. It was theirs.

Jade leaned on the low wall and opened her pink glossy mouth to speak. It paused in a perfect O, before the words tumbled out, one running into another.

'Went up the Centre Saturday, bought a new top, black Top Shop. So I'm in a cubicle in the ladies … '

'Can't go in there.' Jodie rummaged in her bag for her lipgloss.

'Not allowed?'

'No, I can't … you know … *go*. Can't go in a public one – dunno why. Nothing happens, y'know? Can't pee in a public loo!'

16

'Yeah, well, *any*-way, it was like Debenhams not the bus station so it was OK, not gross or anything. Floor was clean. Anyway, like all these girls from the High came in and I was at the mirror doing my gloss and one says, "Do you like my hair?" and I goes "Yeah", though I can't see anything special, y'know? She goes, "'Cos I've just got extensions and shit." I said it was cool, but honestly yours looks way better.'

Jodie had a moment of quiet satisfaction, because she couldn't afford hair extensions, no way, but her hair looked way better than the unknown girl with extensions and shit. Life was good. Jade was her best friend.

She smiled at Jade and offered her gum. The girls chewed in near silence for some minutes, like two glamorous cows. Then the pepperminty bit was gone and they stuck the gum under the handrail.

From where they stood, they watched Tod being escorted across the open space way below by Miss Matthews, the AYH.

Jade yawned prettily.

'I hear he went apeshit in Maths. Whatsisname? Tod.'

'Yeh – told Mr Clark to F-off. Got sent out. Big behaviour bloke got him,' Jodie said in her refined manner.

Jodie didn't use the F-word because her mum had always said only slags used that word, and Jodie cared a lot about what people thought, even though she pretended she didn't. She wasn't a slag just because she came from the estate.

'Think he'll be excluded?'

'No. My mum says they're trying not to exclude people because of targets an' that.'

'He's a weirdo!'

'Fit, though.'

'Nice bum.' They both laughed.

'Yeh, fit but a bit of an idiot.'

'Fancy him?'

'Nah. Bit of an emo.'

The girls stared into space for a while, until the deafening siren sounded for the start of the next lesson. They slowly gathered up their stuff and headed for a last-minute groom in the toilets. Smaller children scattered hurriedly. They didn't mess with Jodie and Jade. Nobody did.

The Assistant Head of Year had a stain on her wall that looked like a lizard upside-down.

Tod was off again. How on earth did lizards have sex? Could they catch Lizard Chlamydia? (After taking E at Lizard nightclubs? The Hot Iguana – Friday nights – girl geckos get in free.)

Tod crossed his legs, then uncrossed them, because it looked weird even to him, and sighed loudly.

The AHY sighed too and looked at him from behind huge, round glasses. She looked for the pencil she had stuck in her hair and failed to find it. She arranged her paperclips while waiting for Tod to say something, as she had been told to do on her pastoral care course.

Tod started to think about Spurs' next match and how he would like an iPhone so he could get an app to listen to the commentary. So she had a bit of a long wait.

In the end the Assistant Head of Year sighed again loudly and sent him on to the Head of Year.

It was like a treasure hunt, thought Tod, *like that programme on TV with the rushing woman with a big bum who went around in a helicopter.*

The Head of Year was a very different kettle of fish to the Mentor and the AHY.

That was a funny expression as well: *kettle of fish.* Why would you put fish in a kettle? Wouldn't the small ones get stuck in the spout?

Sharp black suit, red lipstick, Jennifer Aniston pricey haircut, heavy specs, stressy, no smile. It was the difference between a velociraptor and one of those pink cuddly bunnies on the battery ads.

If Tod had thought he knew what spit was before, he certainly knew now. He could have drowned in it. He could have taken a boat out and rowed home in it. He could have launched a liner …

Well, you get the idea. There was spit. Plenty of it. Rivers. Why hadn't his horoscope said, 'Your lucky plant is buttercup, your lucky colour is maroon and, by the way, wear a mac all day today and take some tissues.'

When she stopped shouting, she said, 'I think it's about time you went on a PSP.'

Tod focussed on a gleaming spot of spit right on the edge of the desk. A games console – surely not? Whatever it was, it wasn't going to be *so* bad; just another thing, wasn't it? PSP? Pupil's a Pest? Purple Shiney People? Prickly Spiky Porcupine? Pizza, Sausages and Pasta? Pizza … *mmmmmmmmmmmm* … pizza!

'It's very serious, Tod. A PSP is a support programme especially for pupils who could be on the road to exclusion. Permanent exclusion from the Academy. This has very serious implications for your future. It would be very unlikely that any other school would take you on if that happened. You would stand no chance of taking your GCSEs. Then what, Tod? Life on benefits, no money, no friends, no purpose to your life.'

(*Living out of bins at the back of McDonald's and a horrible lonely death, drunk and drugged in the gutter,* Tod thought.)

'Are you listening? Sit up straight, please! It's very serious indeed. Seriously serious. Now, I need your parents to come in so we can set this up.'

No way is my mum going to waddle into this school.

'Dad ain't there any more and Mum can't come in.'

'Can't?'

'Ill.'

Don't meet her eyes, don't meet her eyes.

The Head of Year looked at the boy in front of her. Young man, really. His legs stretched halfway across her office. He was slumped in the chair as if he was bored, but his fists were clenched tight and his knuckles were white. His face was closed down and he stared angrily at a point on her desk.

She carefully wiped some spit off the PSP form with a tissue.

'We'll set it up today, but I want your parents to sign a copy. It's, well, extremely serious.'

Sure – that's what's going to happen.

'Now, what are your strengths?'

Football, football analysis, supporting Spurs. I can eat a large pizza in one sitting. And part of a second one. I can average 150 on Wii bowling. I'm a good friend. I control a strong desire to smash things up. I'm unwillingly pure. I may become a monk.

'Like football. In the team.'

Strengths: *Tod is a keen sportsman.*

'Do you do anything worthwhile? Community service? Charity work?'

Shall I tell her about Ed? About helping Mum to decorate the nursery? About the Shoe Shop from Hell?

Long silence, but she waited him out.

'Nope. Nothing.'

'And what do you need to improve on?'

Would like to get my bowling average up to 200. Need to find someone to do my Maths homework. Want to get to know That Fit Girl down the Road. Stacey? Macey? Not Tracey, puh-lease!

'Want to do well in school.'

'And to achieve that you have to … '

'Be good?'

21

Targets: *Not to disrupt Maths lessons.*
To do my homework on time.
To actually give it in.

'Is there anything else you want to say?'

Aaaaggggggggggggggghhhhhhhh! Tod heard the silent scream echo round his head.

'Nah.'

The outcome was that Tod was sent to Inclusion. Despite its name, this meant you were actually excluded from anything fun to do until they let you out. It was the Academy's equivalent of maximum security prison.

In his bag was the PSP which he could carefully sign with Mum's name that evening and take back to school. In Ice (as the pupils more accurately called it, as it was really cold in there) a huge, gigantic, unsmiling male alien called 'Mr Selby, sir' gave you English worksheets all morning and Maths worksheets all afternoon. The walls were covered with motivational posters:

Everyone is good at something.
Your behaviour is your choice.
Kindness shows strength.

They were superglued up there because otherwise the pupils stole the blu-tack and threw it at each other when the teacher's back was turned, or they stuffed it in the power sockets.

Tod was actually very grateful that he had not been excluded from school, which would no doubt have brought floods of tears and a lot of yelling from Mum. He didn't want her upset at the moment. Well, actually, Dad had done a pretty good job on that front, going off with That Ugly Cheap Young Tart With The Tight Blouse From Accounts, but he didn't want her any more upset.

Tod had absolutely no desire to take a step on the road towards permanent exclusion. He didn't want to be educated in any sort of a unit. The guys who were, waited around at the school gates on their bikes with their sad faces and their sad little cigarettes and their sad swearing every other word. If their lives were so great in the Pupil Referral Unit ('in the ****ing PRU'), why did they want to hang around outside the school gates? No, Tod liked being educated with his mates and didn't usually mind his school, especially soccer lessons.

He watched his class trot out onto the school field with a sigh and traced around an ink mark on his desk that looked like a rabbit.

He knew how rabbits had sex – he used to keep them. They only had to look at each other across the garden and wiggle their cute little pink bunny noses. Tod had kept two females and he ended up with fifteen.

With any luck he could keep this sorry episode secret from his mum. He must remember to examine the post each morning for a while. At least he would miss the homework.

The small ginger kid next to him was in for taking all the door handles off the doors in C block. He had a huge pile of them in his locker apparently, which had been discovered during a routine drugs bust.

Tod watched as the kid tried to unscrew the side of his chair.

Tod carefully signed his PSP (Pretty Stupid Paper) twice and put his hand up.

'Got an envelope, Mr Selby, sir?'

The ginger kid's chair collapsed and he fell onto the floor, where he lay sadly twitching. Mr Selby-sir ignored him. He stepped over him as he walked down the room to Tod.

And again as he walked back.

In her office the Head of Year carefully painted her nails red. She liked doing her nails in school time. It made her feel naughty.

She held her hand out and blew on them.

Nice kid, she thought. *He'd be alright. Probably. Maybe. Oh well ... Should she buy a kitten at the weekend? Was Dexter on tonight? She might go to Marks and Spencers on the way home and buy pink fizzy wine and chocolate ...*

When her nails were dry, she sent an email round to everyone saying Tod Mortimer was on a PSP, added him to various lists, got up and wandered down to the canteen. Fish and chips on Friday.

Tod stretched his long legs out under the tiny desk in Ice. He'd been brought a sandwich because he was being punished and was not allowed to eat in the canteen. As if he cared!

The smell of fish and chips wafted up the central air vent and Tod dug his pencil into the desk. It snapped.

He was glad he could go and tell Ed about it all after school. He hoped Ed was feeling better, because Tod really needed to unload.

Yes, Tod thought, comforted by the fact. *Ed would make it alright again. He always did.*

That would never change. Ed was the one thing in his life Tod could count on.

*In which Death pays a visit
and Tod gives a friend a lift.*

Tod ran out of school as if all the Mentors and Heads of Year in the world were chasing him in a bizarre Mentoring Race: *Ready, steady, go – but don't try to win in case you upset someone!*

Straight on the bike and down the hill, wind blowing the day out of his brain.

Shame Ed couldn't do that, he thought.

Ed was in a high security block of his own: the Sunset Nursing Home for Gentle Folk. Not that there was anything gentle about Ed. Tod reckoned he must have been sent there by mistake. Like when Mum spent the whole day looking for her MOT in the filing cabinet and Dad had put it under 'C' for car. Somewhere there was a sweet little old lady in a home for Ageing Juvenile Delinquents wondering how she got there. And here was Ed, in the Sunset Nursing Home for Gentle Folk, sitting chatting up the nurses in his Guns N' Roses T-shirt and faded blue jeans.

Tod had first met Ed on work experience. Tod had wanted to help at the fire station for his work experience, or be a mechanic – or perhaps help out on the golf course. Trainee astronaut would have been good, too. Then he got a really bad cold, missed three days at school and got left off the work experience list.

So he got the nursing home.

He hadn't minded the nursing home, though. Tod quite liked old people. They were nearly all irritable and really rude, and some of them were even a bit violent – but then so would he be, cooped up all day with a load of old people.

It was funny, though, how old people didn't seem to like other old people at all. In fact they didn't really think they were old. They thought they were in there by accident and it was all a mistake. They were innocent! Even though the Sunset Nursing Home for Gentle Folk was a really posh nursing home, they nearly all felt they had been cruelly abandoned by their families.

No fun being abandoned, Tod thought. He hoped his father was having fun with That Slag, because no one in Tod's house was laughing.

Tod punched the code in and walked in. The heat and the smell hit him immediately. It was disinfectant with undertones of talcum powder and lavender – and just a touch of wee. The thermostat was permanently on the 'Amazon Rain Forest – Blooming Hot and Sweaty' setting, because the Oldies had no energy to waste in keeping warm. They were using it all just to stay alive.

It was dead strange. It was very quiet that afternoon. There was no noise at all. Tod could hear no radios or televisions. It was too quiet, in fact. He had only been there once or twice when it was this quiet – and both times someone had left in an ambulance and not come back. Actually the home was too posh for people to die – they 'passed away', and then they weren't dead – they were 'resting' or 'at peace'.

Both times when this had happened before, the Oldies had been sitting quietly in their rooms, thinking beautiful thoughts of the departed one. To be honest, Tod suspected that they thought that if they all sat in front of 'Richard and Judy' with the sound down, the Grim Reaper would be fooled into thinking they were at the chiropodist and p*** off home for a cup of tea.

So who was it who was at peace this time? Some of them had been in God's Waiting Room for so long they must have been wondering if they would ever get to see the big 'G' himself.

Tod would ask Ed, who was at the head of the queue for Heaven. Ed always knew what was going on. Tod bet he would have dug out his Grateful Dead T-shirt just for this afternoon. Or he might have broken out of the place for a fag, until all the fuss died down.

As Tod came round the corner towards Ed's room, one of the senior nurses, Sophie, was bustling in the opposite direction with a tray. She was a lovely woman of about thirty and seemed to Tod to be as soft as the sound of her name, all generous curves and generous thoughts.

Normally her eyes lit up when she saw Tod and, after he had seen Ed, she would talk him into chatting to some old biddy, or ask him to lift stuff or give something a good clean. Sophie had given Tod a brilliant report after work experience and, just for a brief couple of days, everyone had been pleased with him.

Today she didn't meet his eyes, and the first feelings of anxiety started to stir in Tod's stomach. An ache started at the back of his head, and if he didn't have butterflies in his stomach, at least he had something smaller – a few moths perhaps.

'Hi, Soph!' he said quietly. The silence was swirling around like a ghost in the corridor, muffling his voice. 'What's happening?'

'Tod, I'm glad you're here,' Sophie said. 'Can you come through and talk to Ed?'

Something in the way she said it made Tod know it was not going to be his usual sort of chat with Ed. He wasn't going to be talking about Ed's travels in Marrakech, or the time Ed took his camper van across California. Ed wouldn't be trying to get him to smuggle drink or ciggies into the Sunset (as Ed called the home), or pictures of under-dressed women. (Ed was obsessed with Mariella Frostrup and was convinced Tod could get pictures of her in her bra and panties on the internet).

The moths started munching at Tod's stomach lining and doing a bit of poorly practised formation flying, banging into each other.

Was Ed ill?

Yes, Sophie nodded, her voice all trembly. Something had happened in the night. The doctor had been with Ed most of today.

They had tried to send for Tod at school, but the secretary hadn't been able to find him in his usual classes.

Ed's room was Sahara hot, but Ed was covered up with sheets and blankets. A huge nurse Tod had never seen before stood by the window, blocking out the light.

Tod had never seen Ed propped up like this before. Ed loved his bed and often, just to pee people off, he wouldn't get up all day, even though he was perfectly OK. He would sit there surrounded by his laptop, his iPod and books and magazines, and demand meals in bed which he then spilled all over the sheets (which always seemed to have egg stains anyway). He would be sitting there, shouting and laughing, swearing every sentence, flirting with the staff, making loud phone calls on his mobile, selling and buying shares, probably arranging revolutions in small African countries and waving his arms about as if conducting a small and stroppy orchestra.

Now Ed looked so small, so very small and still, tucked up and tidy. He didn't look so grey against white sheets, and he'd never looked so very, very clean.

It really was very hot. Tod felt ill. Ed's usual smell of smoke and joss sticks, pub and sweat was completely gone. There was a sickly-sweet smell of air freshener in the room.

Tod sat on the bed and spoke to Ed.

'What's going on, then?'

'Not – *huh* – in lessons, Tod? *Huh – huh*. With a girl?'

Every word was difficult for Ed to get out, Tod could see. Ed was making a horrible sound instead of breathing properly.

What had happened? How could this just happen? Admittedly Ed had been slowing up a bit – well, a lot. A bit off his food, and he'd been in a really foul mood recently. But this? What was this?

'Got chucked out of Maths, so they put me in Ice.'

'Nob,' said Ed. Then he closed his eyes and took some deep, heaving breaths. There was a long silence while Sophie, Tod and the huge Nurse listened. Then Ed opened his eyes and smiled.

'Don't … be … a nob … forever,' he said.

His eyes closed and the nurse, who had the kindest and prettiest eyes Tod had ever seen, nodded to Sophie in a sort of secret, 'We know what will happen now,' – 'No need to say it' – way, and Sophie put her arm round Tod and guided him out.

Tod sat in the corridor looking at a dried flower arrangement on a silly little table, trying to remember a prayer, any prayer at all, for the next twenty minutes.

He couldn't remember 'Our Father' because he hadn't really said it since his first school and he kept getting stuck at the 'trespasses' bit. He remembered he used to say, 'When I lay me down to sleep' when he was little. He knew it all the way through, so he started muttering it over and over.

Sophie came over to him, rubbing her eyes.

'I'm sorry, Tod,' she said simply. His mind tried to process the words. They were never good words, were they, in this context? When the camera panned out and the handsome young doctor said those words to the bawling young mother or wife and her small cute child, we all knew what it meant, yeah?

Then, 'We did all we could.'

He'd seen it on Grey's Anatomy. It meant the unfortunate patient was still in twenty different red bits on the operating table. Usually with a steel pipe embedded in their stomach.

Tod felt a wave of nausea. Ed just couldn't be dead. He had been so alive. Just a few days ago, Tod had popped in on the way back from the supermarket and they had laughed together about his emergency shop run for his mum's pickled onions and cookie dough. Ed had been wearing his Guns N' Roses T-shirt – the one with impressive yellow curry stains down the front. Tod had eaten two Curly Wurlies and they'd discussed football (Spurs were playing crap) and world politics (the Prime Minister was a nob).

Sophie took Tod's arm and guided him into the little staffroom. He sat down unsteadily in one of the big squashy chairs.

How was he going to cope without Ed? It had been so cool just to hang out with him. Who else would understand him?

Tears started to well up in his eyes and he swiped his sleeve across them, almost before Sophie could see them.

'I'll just go and get you some tea.' Sophie bustled out.

Tod sat and picked at the hole on the chair's arm, trying to make it into the shape of South America. He felt a bit numb really. It was turning into a very rubbish day.

That was when the voice first spoke in his head.

It was Ed's voice, an angry Cockney, and it was lodged in a spot very definitely just above Tod's ear.

Not as rubbish a day as I've had. I was going to watch that Clint Eastwood film tonight. And I'd got Soph to put a bet on for Saturday. Bet it flippin' wins …

I don't see why *you're* so upset. I'm the one that's dead. That's pretty final you know – no popping back for a pint with the lads. It was a great body at one time. I did a lot in that body – I could tell you some stories – and now they're just going to chuck it away. They may burn it and scatter it. Hope they don't leave me in one of those Gardens of Remembrance surrounded by smelly plants ...

Could you take me to a club with you instead and just forget to bring me back? My body probably still all works as well – except the heart, obviously; that was a bit of a let-down. The rest of it seemed OK, though. Well, the feet were a bit past their best and I did have a mole on my never-mind-where that I was a bit worried about. Just goes to show it's not worth worrying, doesn't it? Worry about a mole and then your heart stops! Got to laugh really ...

Anyway this is a bit of a turn up, isn't it? Dead. I was expecting beautiful busty blonde angels, fluffy pink clouds and heavenly choirs, glitter everywhere ... a cross between Christmas and a Philadelphia advert ... God telling me I'd done a great job (except for forgetting to feed the goldfish that time and, of course, Marie) ...

But I seem to be stuck here – in your head – just above your left ear. Bit odd. Bit "Night of the Living Dead", really. Bit zombie-esque ...

Tod, you *can* hear me, can't you? I'm dead and I'm stuck in your head. Tod? Tod?'

OK, Tod thought. *Don't panic. This is probably just shock. I'm just having a very peculiar reaction to the news. I'll just sit here a bit and wait for it to pass. No need to panic, just because I have a dead person stuck in my head, talking to me. Happens all the time.*

So can I go to my funeral? That'll be really neat, I bet. All those little blonde grieving women in black, mopping their eyes with lace hankies under black veils. I can't actually think who, but perhaps you could find

33

some? We could advertise in the Chronicle and Echo! You only die once, after all ...

Can I have rock music? The Stones, of course. I know - what about, "Hope I die before I get old"? That was The Who, wasn't it ... except I *did* get old, of course, so perhaps not ...

Hey Tod - can I go running in your body? It's really cool. I bet it works great. Tod? Tod? Are you listening, Tod? Oh - oh - I've just thought ... do you have a girlfriend?

Tod hummed a little tune quietly under his breath. Some bloke had come into the school and taught them to count to ten in Japanese in order to get good GCSEs. Tod hadn't quite understood how that worked out, but he decided to try counting in Japanese in order to block out Ed's insistent voice.

Then he tried reciting his seven times table until he got stuck at around eight.

Tod drank Soph's sweet, weak tea gratefully, with Ed exclaiming just above his left ear how good every mouthful tasted. Then finally, because he didn't know what else to do, Tod got up and cycled home, with Ed singing,

Knock, knock, knocking at Heaven's door,

loudly and off key in his head.

'Hi Tod!' his Mum called as he came through the door. 'Have you had a good day? Anything happened? Did you forget your Maths homework again? That pretty girl down the road dropped it off.'

'Not really,' Tod called, answering all the questions at once, and thumped upstairs to his room before she could tell him about her swollen ankles or her water infection.

Heaving a load of freshly laundered stuff off his bed onto the floor, he threw himself down on the duvet. He stared up at the small stain on his ceiling that was shaped a bit like Jordan, or at least like two bits of Jordan (the model, not the country).

What was he going to do now? In fact what *could* he do now? He was being watched all the time – and nearly all his favourite activities involved being alone.

That's a bit sad, innit? Get up, Tod, I need to pee.

How can you need to pee, Ed? You haven't got a body.

Oh, perhaps it's just – you know – all in my head.

You haven't got a head – it's my *head. You need to pee in my head! I'm not even going to think about that! You're only sharing my head until you go knocking on Heaven's door. So don't go peeing in it. Aren't you supposed to go into the light or something? This may be news to you, Ed, but it's a bit weird having someone sharing your head. I mean, it's not like it's a sandwich or a bungalow.*

Can we have a pizza, Tod?

Do you smoke?

Wanna go for a run?

Swim?

Come on, Tod. I've been old for a long time. I want to live a little.

In that case – you can do my Maths homework. If you wanted excitement, you should have leapt into a professional footballer's head, or a skydiver or something.

In the end that was what they did. Ed polished off the Maths homework in about twenty minutes, explaining it as he went along in a tone that clearly implied that Tod was a moron. You did the brackets first, apparently. Why hadn't the Maths teacher said that? Writing BODMAS didn't really help, did it? What was he, a code-breaker?

Then they watched 'Shaun of the Dead' on DVD in Tod's room, with Ed nearly wetting himself laughing. (Well, in a manner of speaking.)

Tod went to sleep strangely happy. Although he had a dead guy in his head, he had done his Maths homework on a Friday night, which he had never done before. Or on any other night, to be honest. Or any other homework.

And it was quite nice not being alone any more.

THREE

In which the shoe fits
and Tod decides never to have sex at all. Ever.

Tod woke up at about eight o'clock to go to his Saturday job, which was a shame because Ed was awake at six.

At seven they were both up, cleaning the kitchen (Ed's suggestion), drinking dark brown tea and singing some song about it being a long way to Tipperary. They took a cup of tea up to Tod's mum, who heaved herself up in bed like a small elephant and sipped it gratefully.

She's huge, Tod thought. She virtually had her own time zone. How many babies were in there?

If it was all water, he hoped he was well away when she gave birth. Tsunami, nothing. Run for your lives! Get to high ground!

'Were you cleaning the kitchen?' she asked, her eyes narrowed and suspicious. 'Were you sick in it or something?'

Talk to her. She's not happy, Tod.

I flippin' know that. Would you be happy if you weighed the same as a hippo? And, actually, looked a bit like one too. Talking's not easy though, is it? They're not interested in good stuff like PS4 games or football. They want to talk about your feelings, or how you're doing at school, or your plans for the future.

'Nope, Mum, I don't do cleaning.'

Tod and Ed didn't really get on that well together. Ed, being old, was full of energy and a desire to put the world right, mainly by cleaning it bit by bit. Tod, being young, was very tired and wanted to lie on the settee and watch MTV for hours on end.

It was strange, though; it might only be a first reaction, but Tod didn't mind Ed being there. He didn't have to talk to him – somehow Ed seemed to know how Tod was feeling without all the boring talking. He was probably listening in.

Having Ed there made Tod feel he could ask for advice. He had lost a sort of sore feeling in his chest. It was funny. He hadn't realised he'd felt rubbish until he felt better. Thinking about it, Tod reckoned he had felt a little bit choked, a little bit down ever since dad had gone off with that Common Slut I Bet She's Not Even Really Blonde I Wouldn't Be Surprised If She Was Half His Age, six months ago.

There was a good feeling about Ed being there. He made Tod feel happier, like nothing mattered too much. Tod supposed nothing did matter too much once you were dead. It was kind of a biggie to get out of the way, really.

Obviously Ed couldn't stay there forever – for example there was the Fit Girl Down the Road that Tod was thinking of getting to know. No hurry though. He had been thinking of getting to know her since they shared a peg in primary school.

Tod just hoped that Ed was actually there and that he, Tod, was not stark staring bonkers. He couldn't see himself explaining to the School Counsellor: 'I hear dead people. Oh yes, the recently deceased live just above my left ear.'

She would be looking for Ed to burst out of his skull, like that scene in 'Alien'. They would lock them both up in a home for bonkers people.

OMG – Saturday was Shoe Shop Day!

I hate today – it's Shoe Shop Day. I work in the shoe shop!

What do you hate about it?

I work.

Anything else?

In a shoe shop.

Anything else?

What's not to hate?

So what's so terrible?

Sweaty feet.

Bending down.

Smiling all day.

Measuring kids' feet.

Kids.

Feet.

The Ginger Manager hates me. And he knows my dad. And

That Slapper, he knows her too. They probably go on holiday together. Ginger freak!

The other assistants hate me because I'm the Saturday Boy.

Tod carried on with The List. He had thought about it a lot. Every Saturday.

Being called the Saturday Boy.

Being teased because I don't sell any shoes.

The storeroom.

Spiders.

Dirty coffee cups.

Not being able to think.

Not understanding what women mean.

Being asked for my opinion.

The look of patent.

The feel of suede.

Not being allowed to work the till.

Everyone can hear when you're in the toilet, so you have to pee really quietly.

The nylon carpet.

Electric shocks.

Wearing a name tag.

The Ginger Whinger telling me to try harder.

Did I mention sweat?

Kids?

Oh, and shoes. I really hate shoes. I hate their nasty names: loafers, kitten heels, flats, stilettos, sandals, trainers, crocs, starter shoes, gro-right shoes, patent, suede, two-tone … I hate shoes.

You're very suited to the job then?

Hate it.

Get another job. Play in a rock band.

Sure – I'll give Coldplay a ring. Look, Ed, if I get another job on Saturdays and I hate it, right, then it's me, not the job. Better this way.

That makes no sense at all. Ring the Stones – they're bound to need a replacement soon. They're as wrinkly as I am. Ah. As I *was*. Sorry – still getting used to it.

Really though, it wasn't so bad with Ed there. Tod found some of it quite funny. It was Ed's comments and the sound of him chuckling away, just above his left ear.

Ed gave each of the shoe-shop customers their own nickname: Horseface, Shouty Guy, Drop Dead Gorgeous Girl, Mobile Phone Ear, Bald Smelly Under Arms Bloke, Anorak Features, Squeaky Geek.

Tod saw the funny side: like the kid with the ice-cream who transferred the contents of his nose onto the raspberry topping before offering his older sister a lick. Then he decided he didn't want it (not surprisingly really as it was covered in snot) and gave it to his mum, who absentmindedly ate it whilst the little sister tried on shoes.

Ed also made a bee-line for every female customer, especially those with a short skirt, and he tried to persuade Tod to look up it. Tod had to stare at the feet. Only the feet, only the feet.

He found he had to concentrate really hard not to say out loud anything Ed was thinking – but he couldn't help smiling. Then his customers smiled back.

Ed was not even inappropriate. He was *dead* inappropriate. He was also quite a good salesman and Tod made no end of sales. He could feel the quiet hatred of the other sales staff bearing down on his back, and it made him happy and his heart sang.

Then there was an incident.

Tod lost control of Ed. He just took over.

At five twenty-five exactly, a really heavily-pregnant woman tottered into the store. Everyone started to tidy up the racks, dust the counter, dash for the loo. Nobody wanted to serve her just as the store was closing. Perhaps she would totter right back out. They lined up at the door to give her a bit of a hint. She collapsed sighing onto a plastic bench.

They looked at her.

She looked at them.

They looked at her.

Then Ed did something very weird inside Tod's head. It was like a nudge. It hurt and made the floor shift about like an earthquake. Like a mental elbow.

Tod moved quickly to serve her – he didn't want brain damage. Surely it couldn't be healthy to have someone nudge your brain.

The woman pointed at the comfortable great boots she wanted to try on. Then Tod couldn't get her second shoe off. She couldn't see past her huge baby bump, but her feet had swelled up in her shoes and now her shoes were stuck on.

She started to apologise: 'Sorry, sorry.'

Tod pulled and strained. The other sales staff watched him, laughing and snorting. He pulled with all his strength – and finally the shoe came off. He fell over backwards, like some wimpy Prince Charming.

42

He was laughing himself now, but as he fitted the second shoe, what felt like a raindrop fell on his hand and he looked up to see her eyes filled with tears. He felt himself go red. He hated it when women cried. Just lately his mum sprang a leak every five minutes.

Tod heard Ed say,

'Don't cry, you have really pretty feet. It'll be OK again soon.'

Only Ed didn't say it. Tod had said it out loud.

Tod was just keen to have her served and out of the shop, before she popped out the sprog next to the reduced handbags. But when he saw her smile, he supposed he would want people to be nice to his mum. Fair dos, really.

She gulped a bit, like a huge, soft frog, bought the shoes and waddled out of his life.

The manager, who had hardly spoken to him before, was really taken with Tod's kindness and 'exceptional customer service'.

I've been thinking,

Ed said,

I used to run my own business when I was alive. Why don't we offer them a cooling footspray? Maybe the customers would like it and it would stop a bit of the niff? And lollipops for the kids, but only if we sell them some shoes?

Dutifully, Tod relayed these suggestions to his manager, omitting the fact that he was carrying a Zombie Business Advisor in his skull.

Apparently there were all sorts of health and safety reasons why they couldn't be acted upon, but Ginger M really enjoyed explaining them in his high whiny voice and nobody in the shop got to leave until twenty to six. Tod balanced his annoyance at being late with his pleasure at irritating the rest of the staff, and reckoned it worked out about even, until the manager gave him an extra fiver for 'getting his act together'. Result!

Tod cycled home with Ed whistling something called 'Secret Love', which was horrible.

Tonight was Kyle's party and Tod was really looking forward to it. For years, Kyle's parents had been sensible and responsible. Now they had made the biggest mistake of their parenthood (*so far* – buying him a car was going to be their most expensive mistake), by deciding that, at sixteen, Kyle could be left alone in their three bedroom detached house with all their expensive stuff.

They had gone on a mini break to Prague. They had actually gone out of the country! What *were* they thinking? The word was that he had already killed the tropical fish. He had unplugged them so he could plug in his Wii four days ago. The dishwasher had died in a cloud of bubbles. He had put washing machine powder in the wash drawer and fabric softener in instead of rinse-aid.

As Tod was happily cycling home, Kyle was about to discover that you should under no circumstances get thick toast out of the toaster with a knife.

That evening, however, Kyle was going to throw a party at his parents' house – with girls and real alcohol. He had invited the whole of Year 11 in a huge email that had gummed up the Academy's IT system for hours. (It had also caused a fake fire alarm. Wayne Prescott in 9D got bored trying to log on and went for a wander, out of the open area and down the corridor. Once there, he couldn't resist hitting the fire alarm. It was too easy! The whole school had stood out in the rain for an hour. That Girl had looked really fit with her hair in tiny little rain curls.)

Kyle had put the party on Facebook. (He wasn't very bright. Anyway that was another story.) Tonight, Kyle was supplying music, crisps, alcohol and even some girls.

Tod thought That Fit Girl Down The Road was going. He was going to be there, even if Ed had to come too.

At home, Tod showered briefly. Normally he enjoyed a shower, but it was surprisingly embarrassing with Ed in his head. It was difficult to wash without actually looking at your own body. Especially as Ed had been in the army and knew no personal limits.

Finally Tod had to make it clear there would be no remotely exciting experiences for Ed at all whilst he was in Tod's body. Of any sort. Ever.

Ed was destined for fluffy pink clouds and a harp. Surely he would go into the light at any minute. Was he sure he couldn't see the light, even just a tiny bit? St Peter was calling – try to listen!

Even if Tod had to become a priest for the rest of his life, it was not going to happen. No sex for Dead Ed.

It was a very hacked off Ed who went to Kyle's party that evening.

*In which the flowers talk
in Kilkenny.*

Six months before Ed died, Marie O'Connell wandered slowly down the Dublin Road to her daughter's flower shop.

At that very moment, Ed was opening a new packet of cigarettes on the fire escape at the Sunset, leaning back and feeling the spring air on his face, without a care in the world.

At the same moment, Tod was cycling to school, having forgotten both his Maths homework and his PE kit. His mother was sitting at the kitchen table, sobbing her heart out.

It was a lovely day in Kilkenny: the birds were singing and nest-building and generally knocking seven bells out of each other.

The trees were starting to bud and people were talking about their summer holidays. Marie was hoping to go to the seaside herself. The air was almost as warm as summer, but that little bit fresher. It was good to be alive, and quite frankly, Marie was making the most of it.

She was going to take care of the shop for the day. She wanted to do a really good job, because she knew she had been the last choice. Only after every member of the extensive O'Connell family had been asked and had declined, had her daughter said,

'I'll have to ask me mam.'

'I'll have to ask me mam.' At one time that had been on Lorna's lips every five minutes, but nowadays she said it reluctantly. Marie wished she could turn back the clock. Or maybe just stop it?

Lorna was keen to see her little one in a play at school, and no one else had been free. Even Mick was busy, probably polishing his mirror or scratching his arse all morning – or lying on his sofa leering at that Lorraine Kelly on the telly.

Getting old, that's what it was. Time was, she was at the centre of everything going on. Now, they didn't trust her. They thought she couldn't do it properly, what with the illness, the thing in her head.

She forgot a lot recently and felt off-balance. Everything seemed just wrong, like those TV programmes they filmed with a shaky camera. But it was weird, because sometimes things seemed too real, even though she didn't feel part of it. It was as if she was sort of floating. That gobshite had said that she would burn the place down or something.

It wasn't a very busy shop, but it made a steady profit. The family owned a much bigger place in the middle of Kilkenny. This was much smaller, and she reckoned she could manage it. All the same, even the simplest things seemed to be getting a bit complicated lately, so she mustn't start dreaming. If the place was a heap of ash, lying in between the newsagents and the hairdressers by four o'clock, she actually thought Gobshite Mick (the big auld rockstar, himself) would enjoy saying, 'I told you so'.

She concentrated on getting the right doorway and panicked a bit when she couldn't get the door open, but finally the key turned. It was the right door. It was just stiff, that was all.

It was getting difficult to grip keys, she noticed. A bit fiddly.

Once inside, the flowers greeted her in all their colours, from where they sat in their big metal buckets. They shouted their welcome and Marie said, 'Good morning' in response and dropped a little curtsy to them, then did a little twirl like on that dancing programme on TV. What was it called now?

Marie loved the flowers. The smell was wonderful – heady and exotic, like being in a tropical garden.

The lilies sat coolly in their bucket, watching her.

The expensive roses pulled themselves upright, away from the other flowers. They believed themselves to be too good for the shop and looked down their noses at the others. They thought the daisies and cornflowers were common, because they grew in fields, and they had showed off something rotten when they were put in the next bucket.

Marie's favourites were the big chrysanthemums, like huge balls of gold with thousands of petals. They were friendly and kind and often gave her really good advice. It had been the chrysanthemums who'd told her to try green tea, though. They'd said it did you good and it might help her illness, but it really was disgusting! Still they had very good clothes sense, she found.

Marie started to put the float in the till, but suddenly felt thirsty and a bit dizzy.

'I'll just make a cup of tea, plenty of sugar. That's what I need. Proper tea, that is,' she told the flowers, and went to put the kettle on. Carefully she waited until it boiled and then turned off the gas.

Checked it. Yes, it was turned off.

Sitting down at the counter with her tea, she suddenly felt so very tired. It came over her in a wave and she felt herself doing that dreadful falling asleep and jerking upright thing. She tried to fight it.

'Have a little sleep,' the lilies told her, nodding their heads. 'Just put your head down and close your eyes for a second. We'll watch the shop.'

'Go on. We'll wake you if anyone comes in,' said the carnations. Marie didn't like them – they were cheap, nasty and pink, but she did listen to them. It would be rude not to, and it *was* kind of them to offer. (Nasty squeaky little voices they had, though.)

She put her head down on the counter just for a moment and was instantly asleep. She sank down into the pink cotton wool of her favourite dream.

She was years away and stones lighter! Young and madly in love, she was dancing with Ed in the back garden in Highgate, London. Slow music blared out from a little portable tape player. He held her safely in his strong arms and said he'd always be with her. They would be together no matter what. She looked up into his eyes and saw he was telling the truth. He would never leave her: they would be together forever.

It was so good to feel happy and safe again. The jasmine was in bloom along the rocky old back wall. It had just rained that afternoon, so the scent was sweet. Somewhere there was a heavy buzzing, just like the shop door alarm. It was probably a huge bumblebee. It was a very warm summer's evening and she could actually smell the flowers ... smell the flowers ... smell the flowers ...

She was back in the shop, wide awake and the flowers were talking to her. She listened carefully. They were giving her messages for Ed. She noted them down, so that she could tell him when she went back out into the garden and carried on dancing. She had only come in to get them both another bottle of wine –and then they could dance until midnight.

Mick checked on her at about eleven that morning. At first he was afraid when he found the keys in the lock, but his face cracked into a delighted grin when he saw her, fast asleep and snoring loudly, head down on the counter. A happy little smile was on her lips.

He had been right! The till was wide open and a couple of early customers had even left money on the counter. Stupid old biddy!

He leaned over her and called her name softly.

'Marie!'

Slowly she opened her eyes.

'Ed!'

Mick's face changed into a scowl. His face darkened and he suddenly looked angry and ugly. He swept his long, thick white hair back from his face and leaned over her and hissed.

'Wake up, you stupid auld cow! Anyone could have walked in here. Why don't you just empty the till into the street? Auld and useless! Time for them to put you in a home if you ask me … '

He shouted and swore a bit, and Marie stopped listening to him.

I wouldn't ask you, thought Marie, as her eyes filled with tears. *I wouldn't ask you for anything now, and I never have done in the past.*

'We are shocked,' said the roses. 'Such language! What a pig of a man! Did you say he was a rock star?'

FIVE

In which a house is trashed and Tod is put into a panda car by two huge policeman. (They really do that thing where they guide your head into the car.)

The downstairs of Kyle's parents' house was dark and smoky. Kyle's friends were everywhere. He suddenly had a lot of friends, most of whom were in the kitchen, laughing, swearing and looking for food and drink. Finding drink; not a lot of food though.

Everyone had brought drink, including Tod, who had sneaked out most of something blue in a bottle with tropical palm trees on it. His Mum had brought it back from Tenerife five years ago.

Tod refused the voice in his head clamouring for a cigarette. (*It was OK for him: it wasn't his lungs and he was already dead.* That was pretty much the only ideal situation for taking up smoking.) Tod caved in to Ed's continuous whining,

It may be my last chance!

Tod, how can you refuse a dying man?

(You're not dying – you're dead!) and snagged himself a can of lager. He stood drinking it slowly (he wasn't used to it, really), chatting with the guys who didn't have girlfriends. It was pleasant just to chat with guys who were under eighty. Ed listened quietly, although Tod could hear him practising slang every now and again.

Tod ignored the muttering, chugged his lager, got another, and watched out for That Fit Girl From Down The Road.

Time passed darkly and noisily, and the warring smells of teenage sweat and Lynx built up in the room ...

The goldfish in the lounge hid in its castle as its water reverberated to the music. It came out for a swim, remembered it was scared, went back, forgot, came out for a swim ...

Similarly, Kyle wandered about with a bottle of red wine. He went into the kitchen for a bottle opener, forgot why he had gone in there, wandered back out, realised he couldn't open the bottle, went back in for the opener ...

Kai from the rugby team sat on a coffee table, which at once became a pile of cheap wood on the floor.

In the bathroom a young girl was very, very poorly indeed in the bath. She cried and the mascara ran down her face in thick black streams. Her eyelashes peeled off and sat like millipedes on her cheeks. She thought she would just sit on the loo cover for a few minutes, which she did – and went peacefully to sleep.

Outside the bathroom, the queue built up. Some kind Samaritan started shouting through the door.

Boys, full of lager, gave up and headed for the garden.

People sat on the stairs, smoking, while they queued for the downstairs loo. (The upstairs bathroom had been out of action for quite a while.) Sometimes they flicked the ash into crisp packets. Sometimes they missed. Sometimes the ash just fell off onto the heads of the couple on the stair below.

Tracey Smith, who sat behind Tod in Citizenship, turned the music up as far as it would go. It could now be heard from outer space.

Then Jade and Jodie arrived. They walked into the party like they were walking onto a yacht. They stood posing on their five-inch heels, and some screaming took place. It was necessary to hug all the girls they had last seen on Friday afternoon in Maths. More screaming and fanning the hands backwards and forwards like they do on 'Friends'. Then they hugged again.

Finally, they parked their gum under a coffee table and danced around their bottle of Baileys. Their tiny glittery skirts and tops pulsed apart just enough to reveal their navel piercings.

Every boy in the room watched them.

Every boy in the room feared them.

The music blared. In the back garden it made John Davis, who sat in front of Tod in Citizenship, jump a bit as he looked for a hidden place to take a pee. He felt a bit ill, because he had drunk the entire contents of a bottle that had a bright blue drink in it and palm trees on the outside.

The phone rang in the house, but nobody heard it.

Then the doorbell went several times. Everyone on the stairs yelled, 'Come in!', but nobody opened the door.

Kyle was very happy indeed. He was in the lounge, dancing – all legs – like his dad at a wedding.

In Prague, Kyle's parents sat in a restaurant looking into each other's eyes across a candlelit table.

'He's such a good boy,' his mother said. 'Reliable, sensible.' She hoped it was true. Kyle's father knew it wasn't. His son was an idiot. He offered up a quick prayer to the God of House Insurance and tried to stop Kyle's mother ordering champagne.

In the house next door to their house in England, Mr Freel, eighty years old and very deaf, turned over and went to sleep. The guy in the house on the other side was thirty-two, had perfect hearing and a six-month-old baby, and he called the police.

Tod suddenly noticed That Fit Girl From Down The Road Who Went To My Primary School And Probably Doesn't Know I'm Alive standing next to the food table (bit of an exaggeration – the table containing a bowl of crisps, a dish that had become an ashtray and a bowl of cheesy wotsits).

Even posing with a bowl of cheesy wotsits, she looked cool. She was wearing a very short black skirt and a black top with floaty bits. She didn't look obvious though; no bits of pink stomach. All covered up. As far as Tod was concerned, she could have been wearing a binbag and broccoli.

Perhaps it was the lager; perhaps it was not wanting to chicken out in front of Ed. Perhaps it even *was* Ed. Tod went over and started to chat to That Fit Girl.

Talk about her, not you, that's the secret,
Ed told him.

I learned that very late in life, but it's a trick that works a treat. Pretend you're interested. Really, even if she starts on about Justin Booby or whatever his name is.

It may not sound much of an achievement, but Tod had been trying to build up courage to do that very thing every break-time, every day, since Year 7.

She lived just down the road from him, with what appeared to be a huge family, and had even sat next to him in assembly at primary school. That was because they had been the same height, before his legs had lengthened (and lengthened and lengthened – 'Like Twizzle,' his mum said, whoever he was).

This evening it went just like a dream.

She agreed that the house would be wrecked – such a shame.

Kyle would be grounded until he was forty.

Yes, That Girl ('Lacey', apparently) liked cheesy wotsits (Tod remarked that they make your fingers smell like wee and she said they turned them yellow as well).

She hated Scouting for Girls and supported Spurs. (Tod was massively relieved; he couldn't have continued his interest if it had been Arsenal.)

She even chatted about their striker (he used to be rubbish and now he was brilliant) and the cool goalkeeper for a bit, before Tod remembered to talk about her. Well, shout. Everyone had to shout at each other, probably everybody in a five-mile radius.

She learned kickboxing and was going to do Theatre Studies and Art in the sixth form. Tod was impressed by this, as he didn't even know what they offered in the sixth form. He had hoped to stay on at school, mainly because he thought work was probably a bit of an effort. The clue was in the name.

Tod started to wonder if there was any chance of his getting five GCSEs.

Yes, she was freakishly good at Maths.

No, she didn't hate all the teachers – well maybe one or two. He watched her big brown eyes focus on his face. They had that black stuff rubbed round them and looked huge. The little diamond stud in her nose flashed and she wore big hoop earrings.

She was, no doubt about it, the loveliest person who had ever shouted at Tod.

She looks a bit like Marie,

said Ed.

Who's Marie?

She's dead now.

Well so are you, so shut up!

At least I'm not standing with my mouth open, like a zombie!

Tod closed his mouth suddenly and opened it again to enquire about her kickboxing. Yes, she was quite good. Also, apparently, a brown belt at judo. Tod said she could protect him when they went out … and held his breath.

Breathe, breathe,

Ed panicked,

I've died once this week already.

Yes, she could. When were they going out, then?

The doorbell sounded, followed by a consistent banging on the front door. To give himself time to think – did he have enough money for the cinema next Friday? – Tod went to the door.

There stood the tiniest, most jolly little policewoman in the world. She smiled.

Tod, however, panicked. God alone only knew what was going on behind him. What were they smoking on the stairs?

That's where you're wrong,

Ed laughed.

I know exactly what this is. Someone's having a laugh. This young lady is a strippergram - look at her. Not a real policeperson is she? Look at her cute little face. Uniform's all wrong. Don't be fooled!

This time it was definitely Ed (or maybe the lager) – but definitely not Tod – who stepped forward and playfully knocked her hat off.

Tod was horrified and moved forward to pick the hat up. That was when two huge and very male police constables loomed like liners out of the shadows, blocking the orange glow of the streetlights. Tod found himself helpfully held between them, just off the ground.

His last glimpse of the party was of Lacey's astonished face as he was hauled off to the panda car, protesting and apologising, suddenly aware of being slightly drunk and out of control.

SIX

*In which a small American town is destroyed by a monster
and PC Freeman pretends he is in NCIS.*

So Tod sat miserably in a windowless interview room. Apparently, one of the huge policeman had told him, he was lucky he wasn't in a cell.

He didn't feel particularly lucky.

Apparently, he was going to be charged with assaulting a police officer. They had told him that, as he was juvenile, they would contact an appropriate adult as soon as possible.

They had let him phone his dad, but the call had gone straight to voicemail. Probably in Vegas with That Blonde Little Slapper Whose Skirt Shows Her Bottom She Should Be Ashamed Of Herself, Doesn't She Know He's A Married Man.

So the appropriate adult was going to have to be his mum – who didn't move fast at the moment, if at all.

Tod's head hurt and he was thirsty. He needed the loo but wasn't going to ask. Somewhere at the back of his head Ed banged on about a jail he had once been detained in, in Marrakech. The jails there didn't sound very clean at all and it was making Tod feel even sicker than the lager.

The clock on the wall said it was midnight and the policewoman standing in the corner of the room looked like one of the ugly sisters. There was nothing to do, and if Tod hadn't felt so ill he would have dozed off.

And there were six of us in the band. They put us all in one cell with a bucket in the corner. It was so hot – about eighty degrees. Well, the drummer had just had a curry ...

Tod put his head down and shut his eyes, only for the policewoman to shake him vigorously.

'You might puke and choke.'

'I'm sitting up!'

'You never know – you're obviously quite dim.'

She went back to being a waxwork. WPC Morgan was, in fact, right fed up. She wondered why she always got the kids to look after. ****** sexism, that's what it was. They thought she would be able to talk to him – to 'reach' him. Just because she had a womb, she would be able to communicate with other people's teenagers.

What crap! They should think it through – these mothers all had wombs and they obviously couldn't control their own kids. Look at this one! Great gormless lump! Why was he here anyway, on a busy Saturday night? He was hardly a master criminal.

60

Her feet hurt and her back was going into spasm. It wasn't easy, standing motionless. It got you in the back of the legs as well. She looked forward to going off shift and getting some shut-eye. Pop tarts and bed.

The boy was actually weird. He looked as if he was mentally ill, like he was hearing voices in his head. His eyes kept rolling and twitching, as if he was listening.

She moved away a bit. That was the trouble with this job. You never knew. A PC she knew had been stabbed by a nine-year-old. Bet the kid only got an ASBO thingy, as well.

Should lock the lot of them up in Morgan's opinion, not sit them in the interview room and try to understand them.

The boy looked up and smiled at her. Morgan did her best to show no emotion whatever. Where the hell had Freeman got to?

Tod's mother was asleep on the settee. On the TV screen a huge black-and-white monster, a cross between a worm and a set of false teeth, was terrorising a small American town. One hand (Tod's mother's, not the monster's) clutched a nearly empty tube of Pringles. She snored gently, away in a dream where her husband had come grovelling home to her. She felt his strong arms supporting her and lifted up her face to be kissed.

In the dream she could feel everything was good, it was all back the way it was before. She felt safe for the first time in months. It had all been a terrible mistake and he loved her after all.

The small American town was chomped up by the false teeth, as he said the magic words,

'I'll go to Tesco's for you.'

Again, obviously, Tod's Dream Father said those words, not the monster who was concerned with picking American farmers out of his huge teeth.

She was rudely awakened by banging on the front door, followed by the bell. Followed by banging again. Whoever was there really wanted to come in.

Had Tod come back yet? He had promised to be in by twelve; perhaps he had forgotten his key.

She unpeeled a spit-sodden Pringle from her cheek and tried to heave herself to her feet. As she did so, she noticed that she could, in fact, see her own feet. So that was a relief – because she had begun to doubt that they were actually there.

Third go and she made it. She'd have to stand on tiptoe to see through the spyhole, so that was still going to be impossible for another few weeks.

She opened the door. There was a policeman standing there and a panda car was parked outside (in the road, obviously). Every bedroom light in the street was on. She could see from the policeman's face that it was bad news, and she knew in her heart that Tod was dead. (Which in Germany he most definitely was.)

'An accident?' she stammered.

'No, love. There's been a bit of an incident and he's down the station. We need you to come down there.'

Her emotions rushed from devastated through relieved, straight to livid.

PC Kevin Freeman waited patiently while the woman went to the toilet and then looked for her shoes. Then there was a bit of a lull in proceedings whilst she tried to get her shoes on. Then she had to go to the loo again.

PC Kevin did the silent standing in a corner staring ahead thing. He enjoyed that. It made him feel like Gibbs was interrogating a murderer in the other part of the room. He felt inscrutable and important.

He stopped feeling inscrutable and important when he had to bend down to get her shoes on, but she really stood no chance of reaching her own feet and he didn't want to be still there when the baby came. Then she started crying and he stood awkwardly, patting her shoulder and saying, 'There, there,' until she stopped.

'Don't upset yourself.' *Because you will go into labour and have the baby before anyone gets here and I have absolutely no idea what I would do. It looks messy on the telly and I've just had my uniform cleaned.*

All in all, Tod had lost the will to live by the time his mother arrived at the station.

What will I do then? If you die? Tell you what – why don't you just let me take over? I've never been to university. All that sex, drugs and rock and roll! Bring it on! What do you say, Tod?

Tod's reply was really not printable. He was also going to do his very best to forget the scene when his mother reclaimed him: tears, shouting, more tears, then – even more embarrassing – her hugging him in front of the whole station. It was like the last scene of 'The Bill'.

He could hear Ed's monologue all through it:

Poor girl. Look at her! How could you put your mum through this, Tod? You're lucky your little brother or sister isn't born on the floor of the nick. This is just like Dixon of Dock Green. Used to love that programme. Jack Warner – now he was an old-fashioned copper. Looked a bit like my old dad. Wrinkled face like a basset hound. Dah-da dah-da dah-da dah-da dah-da da da! Lovely theme tune. Bless!

Are those crisps she's got in her hair? Give her a kiss. What's the matter with you? She's your mother!

Turned out the police had absolutely no intention of cautioning, charging or in any other way wasting their valuable time on Tod. They had just wanted to 'give him a scare'. His mother thanked them a thousand times.

'Say "Thank you" to the policeman, Tod. He's really sorry. Say "Sorry", Tod.'

And then they were driven home.

The neighbours had kindly all stayed up until three o'clock in the morning to welcome Tod home. Mr Jones next door even pretended he was taking his dog for a walk.

'Everything alright, Mrs Mortimer?'

'Yes, thank you, perfectly alright, Mr Jones.'

His mother's frosty dignity was a bit compromised by having eyes like a panda. And what were those things in her hair?

In the hall she held him so tightly he could feel the baby kick in protest.

'Don't ever do that again, Tod.'

'I won't. Sorry. Lots of stuff, you know.'

'You spend tomorrow in your room studying. I'll bring your

meals up. I'm going to ask your dad to talk to you, man to man. I can't cope anymore. Understand, young man?'

It was a boring prospect, but at least he had a dead person to talk to.

Fully clothed, Tod put his head down thankfully on to his soft white pillow and was instantly asleep. He dreamed of beautiful, plump young policewomen performing a strip show in front of a huge display of red stiletto-heel shoes.

Whilst Tod slept, Ed slept too, but his dream was dark and scary. He was on a safe white ledge at the moment, but below and all around was the dark. He could see a dark sea swirling and hear the monsters howl and moan. He wanted to stay safe on the soft, white ledge. He was terrified to move in case he fell.

Deep inside Tod, inside his mind or maybe inside his very soul, Ed started to send out little roots to hold on. They were tiny as yet, but they kept growing, looking for cracks and chinks and holds, trying to make sure that Ed could not be shaken off. They were gaining and growing by the hour, pushing Tod over, nudging him.

Tod reached out for the kind-faced policewoman in his dream and she slapped him hard. He moaned and turned over in his sleep, waking Ed suddenly.

Ed stared up at the ceiling in the dark. Tod's fingers were clutching the soft, white pillow. Ed could no longer tell what was real and what was nightmare.

SEVEN

In which Tod gets a death threat, does some Maths
and finds out that Ed killed someone.

Bang! Bang! Crash! Bang!

Either the end of the world had come, or Tod's mum was knock, knock, knocking on his bedroom door.

Tod and Ed slept until midday on Sunday, and would have slept a lot longer if his mum hadn't banged on the door and brought in food on a tray. His mum had worked through fear, relief and forgiveness straight to white-hot spitting anger. Her mouth was set in a straight line and she spoke to Tod in short, hard words.

'Brought you lunch. Eat it. Do your homework. No, do not talk to me! Do not look at me!'

Tod had no intention of talking to her. She looked livid.

'And another thing. You can sort out your Maths today – that teacher thinks you're a moron. He's not far wrong. A police station! Nobody in this house has ever set foot in a police station. *Ever*. And another thing – the whole bloomin' road was watching last night. I'll never be able to show my face at the Indian supermarket again. I have *never*, Tod James Dean Mortimer, felt so ashamed in my entire life. In my condition!

'And another thing. Your baby sister or brother could have been born in a police station. Is that the sort of example you want to set? Is it? *Is it?* I'm waiting for an answer, young man. No, don't talk to me! After all I've done for you. Fed you, clothed you, changed your nappies, wiped your bum. I've finished with you! I'm phoning social services! They can take you away! Take that look off your face! How could you? A police station!

'And another thing – that policeman said you knocked off that young officer's hat. You'll end up with an ASBO thingy! Are you mad? Bloomin' insane? Well, I know it runs in your father's family. They're all bonkers! You are not going to take after him – feckless eejit. That's what they're all thinking you know. "One-parent family – of course he's not cared for. Look at the state of her!" I had Pringles in my hair! Pringles!'

She had gone very red in the face and had to sit on the bed. When she finally took a huge shuddering breath, Tod took the chance to leap out of bed (standing on his bacon sandwich as he did so) and to put his arm round her, or at least as far as it would reach, mumbling, 'Sorry, Mum'.

She pulled herself angrily away from him, got to her feet and stomped out. But he saw the ghost of a smile on her face. He felt better. It was always the same: she loved him too much to stay mad at him.

Blimey! She's OK, your mum. Mine would have knocked seven bells out of me!

Tod miserably peeled a bit of bread and butter off his foot. He noticed there were three new texts on his mobile. One from Lacey:

R U in prison? Wanna file in cake?

She had got his mobile number from someone – and now he had her mobile number! Result!

He saved it carefully to his Contacts three times in case he erased it by accident. Now when they broke up (he could dream, couldn't he?) he would be able to text-stalk her.

There was another message from an unknown admirer that said:

Gonna kick your head in.

A short message, but it said what it wanted to say very clearly. The person sending it was also none-too-bright, because It wasn't signed. Or perhaps it was an ambush? That was worrying and Tod briefly considered replying to it.

Who was stressed with him? This was a new low even for Tod. He was being threatened with terminal violence, without even knowing who was threatening him. He tried to forget it, because there were any number of psychos at school. You could upset them by touching their locker or accidentally tackling them at football or looking at them or breathing the same air in the same town.

The third text was from his dad:

Be outside the flat at six tomorrow. What are you playing at?

His dad had never got the hang of texting, but it was perfect for his unaffectionate way of communicating. 'The flat' was the little love nest above the chemist shop in Wendover Street, which was serving as a home until he and The Bimbo could find a house they liked. It was handy for the insurance offices in which they both worked (when they were not chatting each other up over the photocopier or snogging at the water cooler or whatever things disgusting old people did).

Tod had never got on with his father and really didn't want to have a conversation about social responsibility with a man who had stuffed his own life up in such a thorough manner.

His dad had never really been home that much. He was quite often on the road selling insurance and when he was home, he had seemed a quiet, withdrawn man, not that interested in anything outside of sport on the telly and his daily glasses of scotch. Grey suit, grey hair, grey life.

He certainly hadn't been interested in Tod. Not a bad dad, just no imagination or desire to talk to his son. Friday night bowling had slowly stopped due to other demands on his time. Tod knew now what those other demands were: That Young Slag.

He certainly seemed to have got over his shyness, Tod thought. Maybe not so withdrawn (not quickly enough, anyway – bad joke).

Tod sighed.

He messaged his grounded status to Lacey and asked to be rescued in an SAS-type attack, but her return text just said, *Ha, ha*, with a smiley, and that she would call for him on the way to school.

That simple message caused Tod to punch the soft 'Kenny

out of South Park' on his bed several times in the gut in triumph before drop-kicking him into the middle of the room. Kenny's eyes stared up reproachfully from under his orange hood.

The day dragged horribly. Ed had picked up on the fact that there was schoolwork to be done and suggested that they actually did it. Really Ed was feeling just a bit guilty, in case the whole police hat incident was just a bit his fault.

Tod pointed out in no uncertain terms that it was *definitely*, *positively* and without doubt *completely* his fault and there was no 'in case' about it – *you stupid old man*.

It was against Tod's principles to do schoolwork outside of detention, and he had saved a lot of effort that way. Still, he was really bored, so he decided to give it a go. The only books they had were Maths, and so they did settle down in the end and put in a couple of hours.

Tod was amazed at how easy it was to pick things up when Ed explained them. He always started by explaining just why Tod needed to know it.

You need this to work out how much is due on a loan. The gits always tell you the interest, but they don't tell you that you pay interest on the interest, and then interest on that, until you can't repay it and they send the boys round to break your legs just as you're sitting down to have your dinner. Nice bit of mutton it was.

Then you have to move to Spain and get a job as a waiter in Barcelona, which is not such a great place to be a waiter, let me tell you! Your hands go all red and cracked and the paella is a b****** to get off those big frying pans. I don't think they've heard of Teflon in Spain.

Probability – that's betting, that is. Now this will explain to you why there is no such thing as a poor booky ... Also it explains why so many girls get pregnant. Very useful is probability.

Don't have a clue why this is useful, unless you're planning a moonshot or something ...

Ed also tended to explain things very slowly.

Well, sorry Tod, but you're a bit thick, aren't you boy?

He made Tod note down formulas and methods carefully in a notebook. By five o'clock Tod had absorbed more Maths than he had done in the last five years, and he had an unusual feeling of optimism about the testing scheduled for the next week.

His teachers tested the sets every six weeks to see if, by some sort of miracle performed by the Maths Fairy sprinkling Maths Oofle Dust over them, a pupil had improved so much that they had to be put up a set.

Tod had proudly remained next-to-bottom in the next-to-bottom set since the beginning of Year 7. He was only saved from the last place by the boy who always sat and drew penises on the test paper. Always penises. And always every year.

Lacey was in the top set. Well, that was something to shoot for! He could sit next to her and they could 'work together' (teacher-speak for copying from the person next to you).

In a fit of ambition, and breaking the habit of a lifetime, Tod actually put his homework into his school bag to give in the next morning. Then he texted his mum.

HW done and in bag for tomorrow

and was rewarded by a shouted, 'Good stuff!' from downstairs.

Tod lay down on his bed and stared at the ceiling. He turned over his pillow to the side that didn't smell of lager and sweat. His eyes started to close …

Nice bird, that Lacey.

You shouldn't be noticing. Because you are dead. Not ugly, not old, not even out of the running. Dead. Sorry to be a little bit tactless, but there it is. Dead and cold. Cold and dead.

Yes, that's true. I was just wondering – will you be kissing her any time soon? Because I'm quite good at that too. Could give you a few pointers …

Concentrate, you disgusting old man. Are you sure you can't see a great white light coming your way? Listen – can you hear angels singing? Little fluffy clouds? Or does it maybe feel a bit hot?

I'm only asking because I would like to kiss a girl sometime in my life and I don't want to be a twenty-year-old virgin doubling as a taxi for you! It's between me and her – not me and her and you.

Is that a 'no' then? It's not fair, you know. I'm a bit scared. I've just spent one whole afternoon of my eternity doing equilateral equations. Lacey is lovely, Tod. Remember – I can hear your thoughts. I know you like her. She reminds me of Marie. Can I tell you about Marie?

No. I'm not interested. I'm going to sleep.

I think I might need to tell you. You know, to move on. To go into the light – or maybe the other place.

In that case, get on with it then, but make it quick. And only if there's a chance it might get you out of my head forever. I'm not interested in the sordid details of your love life.

Tell me you didn't kill her.

Well in a way I might have done. I'm not entirely sure ...

What? I've got a killer in my head?

EIGHT

In which Ed confesses all, but is not admitted into Heaven.
Or into Hell – so there's an upside.

It was in the summer of 1960. No, not the Summer of Love. Where's your knowledge of history? I was in Malawi by then – a paramedic, sweating buckets and saving lives. (So actually I think I deserve Heaven – you know, Inn of the Sixth Happiness stuff – but that's another story.)

It was a hot summer, I remember. But then they all seemed hot then. I was twenty-five. It was the year Kennedy beat Nixon in the presidential race. To be honest, I always felt Kennedy was a bit scary. I thought the world was more likely to be destroyed by a bloke who thought

74

he was right all the time than by a guy who acted like a used-car salesman. Would have preferred Nixon. Yes, he was the one who looked like the Churchill dog in the insurance ad.

It was a weird time, Tod. The war was still just at the back of everyone's minds. You talked and worked with the men who had come back from the war. You knew they'd seen things and done things no bloke could get over. Not really.

No fun being a war child either, I can tell you. Would have been a foot taller if I'd been fed properly, instead of powdered stuff. The cigarettes, drugs and alcohol probably didn't help much either. No, not when I was a baby, obviously. Do you think I had a fag on in me pram? They came later and were absolute b****** to get away from. Believe me.

Everyone was waiting for the bomb. The big one. Boom! We were supposed to take the dining room door off quickly so we could hide under it. If the bomb had dropped, thousands of blokes would have died shouting, 'Who's moved that s***** screwdriver from off the mantelpiece?'

What do you mean, 'Get on with it'? You're not exactly going anywhere, are you? Be grateful for the entertainment.

I used to play guitar in this band. Mick O'Connell and The Rebels. Stop laughing! Rebellion was big in those days. Rock'n roll, a few ballads, some harmony numbers – anything we could nick from anyone else really – you call it mashups nowadays. We used to call it swiping other people's stuff and changing the tune a bit. Have you heard of the Rebels? No need to be rude. We were quite big in Ireland – got to number 37 in the charts in 1962 with 'Swinging Baby'.

Trouble was, the whole band was rubbish, but I was a bit more rubbish than the rest of them. Arnie the Agent told them they had to drop me, but I was the only one who understood the electrics and could make the mikes work. Left to Mick and Dave, they would have had to stand on the stage and shout.

So they took me on as a roadie – well, 'sparks' really. I got to travel around seedy bits of the north of England with them. Later, we even did a tour of unpleasant bits of France, the smelly bits of Germany and the really pukey bits of Marrakech. That summer we rented a house in Archway and played London pubs and a few halls. I think Dave was doing an art course somewhere in Hornsey – he painted all the walls of his room black and we never did get the deposit back. Plonker!

I supervised the electrics: wired things up, put out small fires, collected them from the police station (and A&E occasionally) and booked rooms and halls. I listened to them moan about their love lives and the audiences.

Enjoyed it really. The drummer was a bit of a pain, bailed him out of a few nicks in my time, but Mick, Dave and Ali were OK. Usual format: talented one, pretty one, funny ugly one and a thick-as-a-plank drummer. We even gave interviews. The pretty one even had his picture in 'Jackie'. It was a teenage girls' comic – oh, never mind!

Marie joined us on a Sunday afternoon. She was some sort of relative of Mick's and she was visiting an aunt and uncle or something in Camden. She came for tea and stayed for months. She was about my age, but kind of different, you know. Her voice was soft with a sing-song accent. She wasn't pretty – she had a chubby little face – but she was funny and smart. She was forever trying to backcomb her hair. Always had that comb out – quick fizz of hairspray – everyone coughing and complaining.

She persuaded Dave he needed a wardrobe mistress. Mick reckoned she'd had a bit of an argument with her mum back in Ireland. But all Marie ever said to me was that she needed to get away for a bit – she'd be going back, but not yet. So she sewed the costumes back together, kept the drummer away from everybody and dabbed a bit of make-up onto them before a gig. Dave was partial to a bit of eyeliner, but to be honest I think he was that way inclined anyway.

You awake? Well, don't just rest your bloomin' eyes – I'm spilling my guts out here.

Well as time went on we got to be close, Marie and me. In a mad way it was kind of like playing house, looking after four bonkers, smelly children. We spent a lot of time together, keeping it all going. Marie could charm the birds out of the trees – and she had to a lot of the time. Like when the landlord came to get the rent, or the drummer invited a whole pub-full of people home for the night.

They were days of booze, fags and music and we had a great time. Walking on Hampstead Heath (alright dozing on a blanket there) ... feeding the squirrels under Karl Marx's tomb ... riding into London on the top deck of the bus ...

We got to be close and then ... well, you know what it's like being young. Things took their course. You don't have to be crude. Don't use that word, it's not nice – but yes, you've got the idea.

I can still see my room in the house in my mind's eye: Elvis poster, dirt everywhere, the windows would only open half way, big old smelly eiderdown, usually a thumping noise downstairs from the boys practising or someone banging on the front door to complain. A bottle of red wine, packet of Number 6 and Marie.

About midday one rainy Saturday, we were lying in bed together watching the raindrops race down the window, when she told me she was in the family way. Pregnant. Don't you speak English? Bun in the oven. Up the duff. No lead up to it, no warning, just turned over in bed and said, 'I'm having a baby, Ed,' with that soft lilt to her voice. Then she smiled.

Not an unusual thing at all, I know. Not a great tragedy – it happens all the time. But right from the start it was 'a baby' with Marie. Not a pregnancy. Not a 'problem'. Not any of the weasel words I used to make her see sense. It was a baby and she was keeping it – and I had choices to make.

I reckoned I should stand by her – that's what they said in them days. Presumably the standing by her would be standing at the altar making promises I didn't really want to keep. But it seemed that was the right thing to do while she was lying next to me. I should get proper work; maybe my parents could help. We should settle down and save up a bit, live in a semi-detached suburban, pay the bills and mow grass for the rest of our lives.

With Marie next to me, it sounded OK. A bit boring maybe, and I wasn't excited at the idea of a baby – noisy, wet things – but OK. When she was next to me, I couldn't imagine life without her. She said she was going over to Ireland to tell her 'mam', which apparently wasn't easy and was best done face-to-face. We would have to talk about getting married when she got back.

Then it all got serious and I wasn't listening to her. I just watched the raindrops trail down the window and the water collect at the join between the window and the plaster and pool onto the sill. After she left, still nattering on, I turned over and shut my eyes, trying to fight the black, swirling, sick panic in my gut.

Over the next few days I turned it over in my mind. I was a bit up myself in those days, to tell the truth. In my head I turned myself from Rock God to Surburban Dad: Mr Semi-detached – and I didn't like what I saw at all. I didn't want to change my life. There had been talk of a European Tour. I could see places and live a little. The band would become really big and I would be the one who'd left the party too early, who missed out on the money and the fame and, yes, the girls. I would be saving up for a black and white telly so I could watch my friends get in and out of limos. Like the bloke who left the Beatles – a big, fat loser.

Oh, I got myself properly worked up. 'She should have been more careful.' 'She was ruining my life.' Marie wasn't even pretty, I told myself.

I finally thought I would talk to Mick about it. He was the leader and he was Mary's cousin or something. He was also a bit older and a bit of a loner. When you're young I think you often confuse 'cool' and 'wears black a lot' with 'wise'. Looking back I think he was a bit of a poser, but then I thought he would help me – show me the right way of handling it.

I told him in the practice room, surrounded by the instruments the boys abused every day. He took a drag on his roll-up, narrowed his eyes against the smoke and looked straight at me, as he told me that I didn't want to be marrying Marie; she was the 'village bike' back in Ireland. He thought she had even been hanging around with the drummer.

It does really feel like your heart is breaking. Really like there is something wrong in there, an artery exploding or, I don't know, I really don't ... It hurt.

I realised I did love her. So, like the fool I was, I swung back the other way. I had been going to marry her – and look what she had done! She had lied to me and deceived me. Oh I felt very sorry for myself.

Now Tod wanted to know more. *So there was an almighty row with Marie when she came back?*

No, you know blokes don't do that. They don't actually tell a girl how they feel. Do you tell anyone how you feel? No, I thought not. I just told her I needed time to think, but I guess I went a bit cold and she kept on at me all the time. I said I needed space. She couldn't afford to wait, what was the problem? Couldn't we just talk?

Every time I looked at her I saw her with that drummer. I was hoping she had made a mistake, or something would go wrong with the baby because she had betrayed me. Then I would be free and perhaps after a while the hurt would stop as well. You know, I was just ignoring it all, making it go away.

Finally she cornered me and I lost all patience. I told her what Mick had said. She said, 'And you believed him? Ed, you are a fool!'

I said nothing. She came up to me and looked straight up into my eyes. I could see her big brown eyes fill with tears and spill over, running down through the smudgy black eye make-up. Leaving trails like raindrops on the window. She turned and ran out of the house and I never saw her again.

So she went back to Ireland. I tell you what, Ed, we could Google her.

No, that night a girl jumped off Suicide Bridge over the Archway Road. It was in all the local papers. They never identified the body. Mick told me he was notified: it was Marie.

What did you do?

Mick said we had to pull together. He explained he had got what he needed: a roadie. 'For the good of the band, man. We're going to be big, Ed. We need you with us.'

He had lied about Marie. He confessed it all now she was dead. She had never been with another man in her life. I beat the crap out of him, then we went on tour.

That was it? What are you, an idiot? You can't trust what that guy said. We could still find out about her. I bet I could find out on the internet.

No, I reckon I know in my heart what happened. I killed her. We were quite big in Ireland. If she had gone back there, she would have got in touch. All that money she must have needed, and I had it then, still have it I suppose. I know I would have got in touch, with a kid to support. She would have got in touch.

And even if she was alive and we did find her, I'm dead, Tod. I would say the chance for a fulfilling romantic relationship has more or less disappeared completely. I'm dead. Maybe I'll see her soon enough.

There's a cheerful thought. You really lift the mood of a room, do you know that?

Let's get some kip! Telling the truth always makes me tired. That's why I don't do it.

Tod slept, and the Edroots grew slowly but steadily into his very being. Ed lay there, awake, gazing at the ceiling. Suddenly he became aware of something in there (wherever 'there' was), with him and Tod. A switch – like a light switch. Now he wondered what that was for. A switch in Tod's head?

It is quiet in the Sunset Home. The gentlefolk tend to go to bed early and get up early to demand a cup of tea at dawn. Sophie sits at the office computer and sighs. She has a cardboard box of Ed's stuff next to her on the chair. She tips it all out on the desk.

Ed paid his own bills by credit transfer, so she is trying to find out if he had any family. There is a little black book containing phone numbers and addresses, and his office file contains the name of his solicitors. She'll phone them in the morning, because the hospital needs to 'move the body on to its final resting place'.

Apart from clothes there isn't much: a harmonica, a half-full bottle of what looked to be expensive brandy, what she hoped was a tin of tobacco, Rizlas and a small Bible with tissue-thin pages which belonged to Ed's mother at Sunday school in Camberwell. There are some certificates; Ed's birth, mother's death, cycling proficiency, no marriage at all.

There are some black and white photos of various people, some obviously taken somewhere very hot. A group of young people grinning and squinting into the camera; not much vegetation, one scrawny tree.

There is a photo of a very pretty girl bizarrely posing on someone's tomb, it looks like; little summer dress, sticking her tongue out at the person behind the camera. Sophie turns it over: 'My darling Marie, June 1960'.

There are a number of magazine clippings about a band, the young men grinning out of the press photos, confident that fame and money is waiting for them and that they will always be young and cute. 1960 – are they even still alive? Probably old wrinklies, like the Stones or Status Quo.

There are two envelopes, marked 'For Sophie', and 'For Tod'.

Sophie puts them to one side – they need to go to the solicitor unopened – everything must be done properly.

Another envelope contains 'Instructions for my Funeral'. Sophie hopes he doesn't want flamingoes or ice sculpture – she's got enough to do and she really wouldn't put it past him. Betting slips, some rather dubious pictures of Mariella Fostrup. Sophie carefully puts anything with a name aside to try to contact them about the funeral.

The boys in the band might still be a bit famous – she will google them. As for 'My darling Marie', there is no clue and Sophie feels her throat tighten. Sadness for time passing and the final goodbyes to loved ones fill her, and great heavy tears plop down onto the computer keyboard and sink beneath the keys, probably doing the keyboard no good at all.

Sophie put Ed's life back in the box. It was all so sad – best go and eat a nice cream cake, drink a glass of wine and watch CSI.

In which there is a fight, but a ninja saves the day.

Tod's quacking duck alarm clock went off at eight o'clock on Monday morning, leaving, as it always did, five minutes to shower, ten minutes to gel and fifteen minutes to drink coffee.

He jumped out of bed, straight onto a plate of rotting pizza that had moved, surprisingly, all by itself right up to the bed. His phone was lit up on the nightstand and blanking out the sound of Ed shouting.

Where's the bloomin' duck? Your bedroom is a real tip. But a duck? Is there a sheep in the wardrobe? You're lucky you haven't got rats. In my day we were lucky to eat in our rooms. You all sat round the table and had a proper family meal. That's why families break down: no proper family time together. No television in my day either, just the radio. Precious little sex and violence on the radio, let me tell you ... Where is that bloomin' duck?

Yeah, right, thought Tod, *that's why families break down: because they don't eat breakfast together.* He found he was starting to tune out when Ed went off on one.

Tod checked his mobile. He had received eight more death threats, ranging from *'UR gonna get it'* through *'UR dead'* (Ed enjoyed that one) to the more ambitious *'I'm gonna pull your hair out til u die'*.

He had got the idea that someone was very mad with him and there was going to be a fight. And although Tod was well-built and fit, he was frankly terrified. Shit-scared. Tod talked big, but he didn't like fights at all. If that made him a coward, he was fine with it. He didn't like hurting people and, more importantly, he certainly wasn't up for being hurt. He had to lose his temper before he would fight; he couldn't do it cold. Fights were not only painful and embarrassing, but also dangerous. If you went down, surrounded by a crowd, there was a good chance they would start kicking you. Everyone went a bit bonkers. What if some moron carried a knife?

Neither did he like being the centre of attention. This was the worst news, like one of the worst possible things that could happen at school. He gazed thoughtfully at the phone. It wasn't in his nature to get Mum to call him in sick and hope it went away. It wouldn't go away, anyway; he'd just spend a day dreading it.

If he told the teachers, there was no telling what they would do. It was out of your hands then. They could do the weirdest things once they got started, and somehow it would all end up his fault. What if they called the police and the police remembered him from Saturday? Then there was that PSP thing. If they thought he had provoked a fight, what would happen with that?

I could take over. We could do that. You just close down. I've figured out how to do it. I'll fight. He wouldn't forget that. Well, he might if I hit him in the head, but you know what I mean. I'll turn his nose to strawberry jam for him. I've been in a few fights in my time. I remember once in a bar in Georgetown …

Tod let Ed ramble on about some bar fight forty years ago. He knew he could do that. He could give control to Ed. He needed to think it through though. His body would still get hurt and, to be honest, would Ed give him control back? In Ed's position (just above the left ear) he wasn't sure what he would do.

You do know that I know what you are thinking? You'd have to trust me wouldn't you? Come on Tod, you know me …

Yes, that was the problem. Tod did know Ed.

Tod thumped down the stairs and the doorbell went. That never happened this time of the morning. He flattened himself against the wall, like they did on NCIS. It was too late! They had come to get him.

He tried to shout at his mother not to answer the door, but she was already there. He heard her little cry of surprise, but he couldn't see round her. He grabbed the baseball bat they kept in the hall for emergencies and stood braced for attack, his feet wide apart, bat raised. Only to find his mum and Lacey gazing at him with amused expressions on their faces.

Apparently he and Lacey walked to school together now, he heard her telling his mum. His mother was, of course, all knowing smiles and telling looks. He was, of course, awkward and red-faced as he stared down at his coffee. Lacey was, of course, all cool and chat as she sat perched on a stool eating a bit of toast in tiny girlie-bites, looking as if she had been in the kitchen hundreds of times. Just look at the way her little black skirt rode up on her thighs. Her uniform actually looked good on her, black pleated skirt over black woolly tights.

Ed thought so too.

Cor! You're well in there. Get in! I prefer tea by the way. Any bacon?

Admittedly his mum was an embarrassment in her huge pink towelling robe, size of a block of flats, but then the baby was due any day. She was hardly going to look like a supermodel.

This would have been a pretty good Monday if there wasn't a contract out on him. If he was going to walk to school, he wouldn't even have his bike for a getaway. As he left the house, he ignored Ed's snide suggestion that he check for snipers.

'Kevin Turner's going to beat you up,' Lacey stated calmly on the way to school. 'Kevin texted Kyle and Kyle texted Jason and Jason texted Sue – Sue Smith not Sue Spender – and Sue texted Amber and Amber's sort of my cousin, so she texted me. I've texted a few hundred people to check and it's going to happen. He's sort of Kyle's cousin. He says you ruined the party so he's "going to kick your head in".

'I understand from my enquiries that his friends are backing him up. This is what you are going to do. You have to tell a teacher and get it sorted. Go after Year Assembly, just before whatever your option is. Ask to go home early. I'll forge a dental and walk with you.'

Or I could just kick his teeth in.

Whilst she was talking, Tod opened his mouth several times to say, 'But …' He never finished the word because Lacey didn't stop talking, which resulted in his going, 'Ba …', 'Ba …', like a retarded sheep.

'No.' They had reached the pupils' entrance. 'I'll sort it out on my own.'

With me.

'Don't you like having a pretty face and a full set of teeth?'

Lacey considered. No way could he sort it out on his own. He was tall, sure, but he was the softest boy she had ever met. He'd cried when he was hit on the knuckles with a conker in Junior School. The girl he was playing with hadn't even hit him very hard. She couldn't have – she was in the Reception class.

'I'll be alright.' *My face isn't pretty – it's ruggedly handsome – a bit like Johnny Depp. Still, she obviously fancies me.*

Lacey considered. Time for Plan B. Boys needed looking after. They couldn't take care of things on their own.

09.00

Tod in Year Assembly. It's on how to revise.

Staying alive might be a good start.

Yeh, it'd be pretty careless to trash two bodies in the same week. They haven't even buried the first one yet.

You're going to be cremated.

No! That's pretty final isn't it?

I would say that was the least of your worries. You didn't think you were going to move back in, did you? I imagine your body is pretty manky by now, even if it has been in a big fridge.

Leave me alone – I've got to think.

First time for everything.

10.00

Tod is playing football. He's enjoying the game. Ed's enjoying the game. Tod is in defence and Ed's a striker, so they're out of position a few times. It's a brilliant morning and they win three-nil.

In the changing rooms nobody speaks to Tod. His friends are avoiding looking at him. His best friend, Shane, changes quickly and silently and rushes off. Shane is a bit on the heavy side and doesn't usually change in under five minutes, so Tod knows what this means. Shane's scared he'll get involved.

Ed thinks this is dreadful because you stand by your friends, especially in battle, but Tod is not so sure. To be honest, Shane would be about as much use in a fight as Jennifer Aniston. Unless, of course, he fell on Kevin.

Tod changes quickly and looks for Lacey, but she isn't with her usual friends. Apparently she spilt a jar of dirty water over herself in art and has gone home to change. Tod goes to the library and sits where he can be seen by the librarian. She looks extremely surprised, as she's never seen him before and asks if he's ill.

11.05

Ed looks out of the library window at the Science wildlife pond. He must get Tod to order a crispy duck takeaway.

11.10

Tod sits lost in thought in the library. Ed looks for him but can't find him.

Also at 11.10, Jade and Jodie meet up in the sixth form toilets. Several sixth formers protest, but are told to 'get over it' and 'not to be so up themselves'. It is the only toilet in which the smoke detector doesn't work and it's freezing round the back of the Science labs.

The girls light up in a cubicle, Jade sitting on the closed toilet, Jodie leaning on the door. Jade fans the smoke a bit.

'That boy, whatsisname, is going to get battered.'

'Tod. Yeah, after school. You goin'? Watch him get a kickin'?'

'I might, but I'm like really not that into it. That Kevin's a saddo.'

'Everyone's going. Kevin's mates are going to back him up.'

'Yeah, but he's a bloomin' psycho. Psycho with an Asbo. Psycho with an Asbo.' Jade said it again because she liked the sound of it. Like poetry. Like a rap.

'He doesn't need backin' up, he needs a kickin' himself – and I don't think Tod is going to do it. Big Jessie. Big girl's blouse.'

'What's that mean?'

'My mum says it. It means he's a girlie boy.'

'I like him. He's fit. Nice bum.'

'Think he's going to sit down on it pretty hard when Kevin hits him. Was that the bell?'

'Not sure. Are you going to games?'

'Yeah – got a note.'

'Period again? Third time this month.'

'It's the bloke today – he'll believe it.'

They flush the stubs and sling their little pink handbags over their shoulders.

'I hope someone tells a teacher,' Jade says thoughtfully. 'It's a bit gross really.'

'*We* could tell?'

They looked at each other thoughtfully and burst out laughing.

'Yeah, right.'

11.25

Tod's locker is at ground level. The teachers have a policy of giving all the tall kids low lockers and all the short kids top lockers. If you're bullied they like to give you a low locker, so that people can boot you as they go by without having to stretch. There is no appeal process.

Someone kicks Tod hard as they go past. He swings round but they're gone. He can hear mocking laughter as they disappear round the corner of the corridor. A boy he knows vaguely slams into him as he walks down the corridor. Another boy pushes him as he staggers, and he hits the opposite wall. The classroom goes quiet as he enters. He gets the message. He's never joined in himself, but he's seen it before.

11.30

Enterprise. Usually Tod likes this because a) there is little or even no work involved, as the girls boss the whole group about, b) the teacher seems to assume they will all grow up to be Richard Branson and run companies, and c) there is usually a fair chance of some messing about in the corridors.

Tod's group are engaged in making greetings cards which they sell, mainly to teachers, who send them to each other and try to look delighted. Tod is in charge of Divali and as it is now October he is working against a bit of a time constraint. He broods over his sticky card. Nobody talks to him. He talks to nobody. He hopes that light will enter his life like it says on the card, but he isn't holding his breath. He drops the sequins and one of the girls shouts at him.

13.00

The boy who runs the Christian Union says their after-school meeting is cancelled when Tod asks to join. The origami club guy actually comes without even being asked and tells Tod not to think of attending. Shame, thinks Tod, because those guys would be so useful in a fight.

They could pray for a flood, or a plague of frogs, or maybe give the kid a nasty papercut.

Fold him into a large cage?

Forgive him to death.

Fold his legs behind his head and pretend he's a swan?

13.05

A very long lunch hour making a sandwich last, sitting next to the Duty Teacher at all times. Coronation chicken. Quite nice really and chicken was definitely appropriate. Ed rambles on about the school dinners of his childhood and pink custard.

Tod usually plays football at lunch. He misses it. He wishes Ed would shut up. What on earth is spotted dick? It sounds gross.

93

A long afternoon watching Macbeth on DVD races past. He was one mad dude. Tod liked the bit where he said his wife should have waited to die until he had time to care a bit. Way to shift the blame! They ganged up on him in the end and played football with his head.

Tod wonders how he will convert his two or three pieces of knowledge into a grade 'C' pass. Mrs Ellory is his favourite teacher and he considers telling her about the fight. How they were going to play football with *his* head. No – he couldn't do it. He couldn't grass them up.

End of the day

Great. Tod goes to put his mobile in his locker before he leaves: no point in getting that smashed. He couldn't afford a new one.

I've left you money in my will. Quite a lot actually.

Oh, thanks Ed. How much?

Not telling – wish I'd left you the lot as things turn out.

Outside the school, a lot of Tod's year group aren't going home. They hang about in small groups. It is very cold but nobody makes a move. There is a feeling of excitement in the air. Some boys run from group to group and the groups huddle together. It is quieter than usual and there are far fewer girls about. The ones who are there are hanging onto boys. An occasional screech of laughter from a girl splits the silence. No sign of the community police officer and Tod's last hope is snuffed out.

His football mates call over to him, which is good of them

and he appreciates it, but he just raises a hand in greeting and walks past. He's thought about this. His best chance is a one-on-one fight. If lots of people wade in with him in the centre, it will be worse. It's also his best chance of keeping it away from the teachers.

Neither is he waiting for Lacey; he doesn't want her hurt. To be honest, neither does he want her to see him beaten to a pulp or crying, which is an outside chance (but distinctly possible).

Kevin Turner and his mates are by the school gates, and as he leaves they peel off and follow him. Tod follows the school fence round. He walks fast. They walk fast. He walks slow. They walk slow.

Now there are a lot of people following, until a sizeable crowd is at his back. The name-calling starts and a stone hits the back of his head. He chooses his spot, which can just about be seen from the road (and maybe even the staff room) and turns. The circle forms around him and Kevin steps forward. The chant starts low at first.

'Fight, fight, fight, fight ... '

They push Kevin to the front and form a circle round the two boys.

'You f****** w***** '

He's a man of few words.

There you had three of them. He probably knows another ten or so.

'We're here, Tod,'

Tod glances quickly behind him, to see that he is bizarrely being supported by Shane and the Nameless Boys who run the Christian Union and the Origami Club. He feels choked by the gesture. They are good mates, even though he is sure their involvement will decrease his chances of survival and increase his chances of suffering painfully before the end.

'Fight! Fight! Fight! Fight!'

The words are louder.

The crowd is pushing in all the time now. Tod has to stand his ground to avoid being pushed into Kevin.

The other boy's eyes are mad and he's red in the face. Tod wonders if he's actually had a drink. Tod watches him closely for the first move. He can hear his own heart pounding and he feels dizzy. Kevin steps forward, within reach. They are mirroring each other's movements now. Tod is watching for the first blow. Kevin is waiting for him to look away. He knows he will go for Tod's face and then stomach. If he can then get him in a headlock, he can punch and punch. He likes that better – the other boy is helpless then and you can just hurt them. You can see the faces in the crowd while you're doing it, the other boys enjoying it too. He's done it before and it felt really good.

The crowd is still chanting, closed round in a circle of eager faces.

The Deputy Head looks casually out of the staffroom window and sees the mob. *It's a fight,* he thinks. *Not another one!* There is a split-second in which he thinks of the possible outcomes of going to that fight – how he could be hurt, and what his wife will say if that happens. It is only a split-second though, because his job is to protect the pupils. He knows it and he respects it. Even though the teaching website talks about exciting young minds and legally the union tells him he shouldn't get involved without umpteen training courses, he can't let kids get hurt. Even irritating hairy little gits like Tod Mortimer

He shouts across the staffroom to the huge PE teacher (no point in taking unnecessary chances), who grins and leaps up. He thunders down the endless flights of stairs, yelling to staff as he goes. One word: fight!

Several staff are running now, not just the men but women in high heels, PE teachers out in front. They are not going to get there anywhere near in time. Some staff are moving deliberately slowly; they can't face doing this again, but most are making themselves keep moving. The Christian Union pray quietly and the Origami Club finish off a nice swan.

There is a small figure pushed in between Tod and Kevin. Lacey stands between them. They watch each other and sway from side to side, over her head.

'Stop it now. This stops now.' Lacey's clear voice rings out.

The crowd groans. It's not fair – they've been looking forward to this all day.

'Lacey, you'll get hurt,' Tod begs. This is going so wrong.

Get her out of here – this is no place for a woman!

'You f****** b**** .' Kevin reveals another word in his vocabulary.

Hit him, hit him!

Now the crowd is yelling for Tod – just as he loses it. He goes to push Lacey out of the way and Kevin swings at him. Lacey steps back and she jumps and swirls, a blur of black, her hair swinging round in a tight curtain. Her right foot catches Kevin between his legs with considerable force. He folds and goes down with an eerie high scream of pain. There he stays, curled up and sobbing, with the crowd either laughing or yelling at him to get up and fight.

Then there is a frantic whistle-blowing as a PE teacher starts to part the crowd. As if by magic, suddenly there is nobody there. The crowd melts away like snow in the sun, and Kevin is left groaning on the floor, concentrating on the fire in his groin, a horrible throbbing pain.

The PE teacher stomps off in disgust and the Deputy thankfully tries to lug the boy to his feet.

'That f****** hurt,' Kevin sobs.

Tod and Lacey ran together flat out and pulled up panting outside the public library. Backs to the wall, they fought to control their breathing. Then Tod turned to her, bent his head and kissed her.

It was his first kiss, but all the practice with the mirror really paid off and it felt natural and ... well, just as it was supposed to feel, Tod thought. She was warm and yielding and then she joined in a bit and then he couldn't breathe, so he had to stop or pass out. So he did a bit of meaningful staring into her eyes and kissed her again.

Ed even had the courtesy not to say or think or do anything except the mental equivalent of staring into space. Tod had an image of how a dog's owner stares into space whilst his dog is doing a poo. That thought pretty much broke the mood.

Tod noticed Lacey was wearing trousers now. The events of the day came together in his head. *She was quite clever, really,* he thought.

'My ninja girlfriend,' he said softly.

She's a cracker!

Ed agreed.

Can we kiss her again? She's our bird!

My bird. M Y equals MY. My bird. When we are talking about birds: there is no us. No triple dating. You are really old – no, you are dead – that's just wrong on so many levels.

[Sulky silence.]

No, really, it's so pervy there's not even a word for it!

In which Tod discovers some things
he would rather not know.

Lacey was going to do her homework in the library, because she reckoned there was no space at home.

'No space, no quiet, no table to work on, no computer. Can't wait to move out.' Apparently there were five children under the age of sixteen in her house: Lacey, two younger sisters, a younger brother and 'the baby', whom she did not dignify with a gender.

'It's just a baby. Little pink yelling thing. Wet and pooey.'

Lacey's bedroom was only big enough to hold a bed. Even her wardrobe was out on the landing. She seemed very calm about it though, and had been doing her homework at school or in the public library since she was in Year 7. She said the people who worked there made her hot chocolate sometimes.

'They probably think I work there too. I keep out of the way until the little ones are in bed and Mum and Dad are in a better mood.'

Tod was amazed. Lacey had two parents at home – he would swop that for a wardrobe any day.

Tod was going to go straight on to his dad's, but he borrowed Lacey's mobile to phone his mum, because Ed thought he had better check on her.

She was fine – she'd decided to clean out the kitchen cupboards and had found some gravy powder which went back to the seventies and Tod's old Peter Rabbit mug from his baptism. For some reason that had made her really happy.

Tod felt about forty himself as he passed on Ed's advice not to stand on a chair in case she fainted, and Lacey's instruction to have frequent rests and not to 'overdo it'. Luckily the phone cut out before she asked him about Lacey. She would probably trap him and torture him for the details when he got home.

She still managed to ask him loudly to get some haemorrhoid cream if the chemist was open, because … *no, Mum, no details!*

Having saved Tod from the 'jaws of death', as she put it, Lacey disappeared into the library. Her solemn little face was all set ready to do battle with simultaneous equations and the differences between plant and animal cells.

Tod thought she might be some sort of superhero: Got It All Together Girl? Maths Homework Woman? It didn't really have a ring to it, but it would be outstanding if he could get her to wear a lycra costume. He grinned to himself.

Ought to be ashamed of yourself – mucky little devil.

He, on the other hand, scuffed along to Wendover Street and arrived there half an hour early, but thankfully just after the chemist closed.

The girl behind the counter gave him a very funny look as she left. She probably thought he was stalking her.

Tod started to pace up and down the shop, waiting for Dad and That Tart to get home from the wonderful world of insurance.

Three grey slabs, dog turd slab, one white, one grey. Three grey slabs, dog turd slab, one white, one grey. Three grey slabs … ooops nearly … one white, one grey.

All the time, panic and anger in equal quantities churned in his gut. The Coronation chicken had already had an acid-soaked day. He felt really sick. He didn't want to see his dad. It wasn't right what his dad had done. Tod had made a great defence out of not talking about it to anyone. He wasn't going to start now. What on earth was he going to say?

I don't know, Tod. He's your father and you should respect him. And he's family, you know? Blood's thicker than doo-da an all that. Mind the … But he does sound a bit of a pillock.

I'm actually inside this head of yours, Tod. I feel what you feel and I'll tell you, son, it's not natural to feel as wound up as you do all the time. You're full of anger and it has to go somewhere. God knows it's difficult to talk about how you feel, but I think you gotta be straight with him. Just tell him how you feel, or it'll just eat away at you. You don't want to carry, you know, emotional stuff around with you for any time. I think it stops you moving on, living properly. Before you know it you've become a nutter or taken up stamp-collecting. Or both. Or ended up dead inside someone else's head. It happens all the time. Mind that dog turd!

It was OK Ed saying all that, but Tod couldn't – he just didn't have the words and it hurt even to think of talking. It might make him feel worse, and he didn't think he could cope with that. Everyone always wanted him to talk about his problems at school: form tutors, mentors, counsellors. He didn't ask them about their problems, did he?

He reckoned they did it just to make themselves feel better. They thought that if he talked to them, they were doing their job. It was like some sort of contest for them.

They sat in the staffroom going, 'He *really* talked to me.'

'Oh no, he *really* relates well to me.'

'No, no, he *really* opened up to me, *me, me!*'

They couldn't *do* anything to help, could they? How was it any of their business? They couldn't make his dad come back, or make his mum feel less sad.

But look at Ed. In a way he had done just the same as Tod's dad. He had wanted the glamour and the fame, how it all *looked*, all those things for himself – and he'd let Marie down.

His dad was too old for all of this nonsense. Tod should tell him he needed to come home. So Tod paced for half an hour whilst Ed sang a few Beatles' songs and tried to persuade him to start smoking. Tod was good and angry when his dad turned up, alone.

'Alright, Tod?'

'Yeah.'

No, not really. I don't want to talk to you because you've let us down. You should see what Mum's like. You should hear her crying herself to sleep. You should watch her getting really angry and using Language and then apologising over and over.

To make it worse, his dad looked quite happy. He looked better than Tod had seen him in a long while. He whistled cheerfully as he unlocked the wooden door and they climbed the threadbare narrow stairs up to his flat. It was just some rooms over the chemist, but Tod thought they had done it up nice. It was light and airy with plenty of cream paint. It had a pleasant smell, even though the stairs had smelt of cabbage. There were weird things on the wall: bits of cloth instead of pictures. Tod noted with awe that his dad had motorbike parts spread out on the big table. Mum wouldn't have had any truck with that.

'Susan's working late – giving us a bit of privacy, I reckon. Sit down, Tod. Now what's going on with you? Mum says you got in a bit of bother with the police.'

His dad passed him a glass of coke and sat down opposite. There was a silence. Followed by more silence. Silence. Then Tod remembered – his dad could outsilence anybody. If Tod was going for the silence as a means of defence, he would only win if he outlived him. So he went for rude.

'None of your business.'

'Tod, I'm your dad and I love you and you will be my business until the day I die. What's going on?'

Tod could feel the anger building. What a cheek! How could he talk like that? He had no right!

'No, you see, let me explain it simply so you can understand. It's none of your business because you're not there any more. You ran off with your dirty little tart. You left us and now I'm doing it all. *I'm* looking after her and *I'm* listening to her and she's crying on *my* shoulder and you're not there. So don't expect me to tell you stuff, because you're not my dad any more. You're just some bloke living over the bloody chemist shop. You're some balding, sad, old bloke living with a woman young enough to be your daughter. You ran out on me and you're not my dad any more. You left – you don't bloody care about us, so don't pretend you do. And I don't care about you.'

Nicely done, clear but tactful. Are you thinking of a career in diplomacy?

Tod was standing and shouting and it was quite easy because it was coming out of his head into his mouth without him having to think. His dad got up and moved towards him. He was just a bit taller than Tod and a fair bit heavier, and he put his hand onto Tod's shoulder and forced him back down onto the sofa. Leaning over him, his face was puce with rage.

'Don't you ever talk about her like that. You will show her some respect. It's not like that, Tod. You've got it all wrong. Listen to me.'

His dad panted heavily and suddenly backed off, sitting back down and covering his face with his hands. Tod's view of the top of his head showed him that his dad's hair was thinning. When had that happened? He had asked Tod to listen. Tod was listening, but his dad was not saying anything.

'No, you can't tell me what to do anymore. Mum is gutted. She doesn't sleep, she doesn't eat properly. She's the size of a small house. I haven't seen her smile or laugh in months. How can you leave her at a time like this? She can't cope. She's going to have that baby all by herself. *Your* baby, you selfish old sod.'

His dad was breathing heavily. He spoke with his head still buried in his hands. It was almost a whisper.

'It's not my baby. It belongs to that poncey lecturer down at those evening classes.'

Ed whistled softly. The words were out there and they seemed to hang in the air between the armchair and the sofa. Tod could actually see them.

'How do you know?'

It was Tod's voice, but Ed was asking.

Good question, thought Tod.

'She told me. The baby couldn't be mine. We were, what do you kids say? – on a break. Things hadn't been right for some time between us, so no chance. She was proud of it. He was going to leave his wife and family and move in with her. She told me "he was an educated man."

'I was told to leave and, to be honest, I couldn't get out fast enough. He was really educated. Educated enough to emigrate to New Zealand two weeks later. He was probably just ... or ... playing away because he knew he was going. Not so well up on contraception, though, was he? Or perhaps he didn't give a ...

'Well, anyway. I hadn't been in love with your mum for some time, to tell the truth. She sucked the colour out of the world, Tod. She's always miserable, always wanting the next thing. She depressed me from the moment we left the church.'

'Shut up!'

Tod felt like his whole life was a jigsaw in his head. He would have to put the pieces back together, but it would take time. The picture would be different. He wasn't even sure all the bits were there.

Adults were truly rubbish. They were supposed to be in charge and get it all sorted. What a mess!

Wisely his dad did shut up and they sat in silence, sipping coke.

'Can I have my iPod back?'

'Sure.'

'Can we go bowling next Friday?'

'Actually I'm … no … yes … yes … we'll go.'

Tod tried to think of something else he could ask for. Money? Was it worth trying?

There was the sound of lively steps on the stairs and That Tart burst into the room, bright colours, huge lipsticky smile, swishy hair, tiny, tiny skirt.

'Had a good chat, boys?'

You really can see everything in that skirt. It's more of a frill. Or a thrill? I made a joke, Tod, get it? Thrill!

Tod sighed.

'And you're never coming to Consultation Evening again.'

'Agreed.'

Tod didn't know how to leave.

Just get up and walk out.

So Tod just got up and walked out.

Tod ran. He needed to put distance between himself and the day. Down Wendover Street, down the High Street, along the river. It had become dark whilst he was at his dad's flat, and the street lights were reflected in the puddles. There was a faint drizzle in the air, which was turning cold now the sun was down. Geese got up to meet him, hoping for food, and he ran through them. Leaving them behind, their disappointed honks rang comically after him.

Through the park, past the deserted playground. There were not even the usual huddles of teenagers hanging out, sometimes looking for someone selling weed. The world was deserted and Tod's legs pumped to the rhythm of his heart. His headache started to disappear as he got into his stride. The cold air pumped in and out of his lungs. He and Ed were enjoying just running.

Finally he fetched up panting, leaning on a bus shelter about five minutes from home. What was he going to do? He was definitely not going to 'get things out in the open', as Ed had suggested. How could he face his mum now? What about the baby? It belonged half to his mum and half to some ceramics lecturer in Wellington (heartless git).

There was a full sky of stars and the moon was out. He felt good from his run and his fight problem seemed to be solved. In fact, remembering how Lacey's leg kicked out and her precise height in relation to Kevin, he wondered if the boy would ever walk straight again – or father children for that matter. That might be a good thing. He was really dumb.

Then Ed wanted to do a bit more running, so Tod set off again through the early evening mist. Running was easier than thinking, any day.

Lacey lay on her bed with her headphones on. It was a good job she was short, because her dad had sawed off the end of the bed to get it into what was essentially a large cupboard. So the actual end of the bed was propped up with bricks.

It was handy really because Lacey could look out the window and keep an eye on what was happening on the landing at the same time. It was also right next to the loo and had the continual noise of running water, which Lacey pretended was a mountain stream or a waterfall (depending on the state of the plumbing).

Thoughts were running pleasantly through her head, to the sound of the Ting-Tings. Tod – what was he like? Kevin would have slaughtered him. As for Shane, they would still have been scraping that lard-arse off the pavement.

She smiled slightly in the dark as she remembered Tod's naked fear of violence. He was a weirdo – not quite there really, but he'd do. He definitely had potential, and he wasn't boring. He had asked her about herself, which was always a good sign. He was easily organised.

She was glad she'd got the Maths homework done. Her PE kit was packed up on the landing for tomorrow. The cake ingredients were in the kitchen with a notice that said, 'Do not eat these raisins or you die!' propped up next to them and decorated with a small skull and crossbones.

In the morning she would collect Tod on the way to school and start to mould him into a decent boyfriend. It was all sorted.

To think he had thought she was called Tracey!

'That's not my name,' she sang quietly to herself. 'That's not my name.'

He would not know what had hit him.

Tod let himself into the house at about nine, braced for the 'Where-have-you-been-I've-checked-and-you-left-your-father-hours-ago,' conversation. He just wanted to avoid his mum for a bit until he'd got over the latest shock-horror revelations. At this rate it would be a wonder if he didn't start acting up, get excluded from school and spiral down into a hell of drug addiction and unemployment like in the Daily Mail.

His mum was fast asleep on the settee. On the telly, David Attenborough was explaining something earnestly to camera, apparently balanced on a volcano holding a terrified lizard.

Tod turned him off and went and locked up.

She'll be cold when the heating goes off,

Ed remarked.

Tod thought this was rich coming from a bloke who threw the windows open every chance he got. He went and got the Buzz Lightyear duvet from the spare room and threw it over his mother.

He noticed she had Pringles in her hair again.

What could you do?

ELEVEN

In which there is a tsunami.

Tod woke up without the alarm on Tuesday. Nor did his mother shout dementedly up the stairs to him like a banshee on drugs. There was silence in the house. It crept into the corners of his room and sat there with the spiders and the small balls of fluff, being unnatural.

An unnatural silence.

Where was she? Had she overslept?

He lay with his eyes open for a second, looking at Jordan.

Have we got time to have ... ?

No! I've been very clear about that.

Just wondered – but you haven't got a long-term
plan on that one, have you really?

I've got a policy, Tod thought as quietly as he could, but there's
no doubt it was a problem. *How long did Ed say he was staying?*

I heard that.

The house was quiet. No radio downstairs, no movement.
None of the clanging of cooking thingies and off-key singing of the
Abba songbook with which his mother usually greeted the morning.
He remembered: his mother was about nine months pregnant.
Perhaps he should investigate …

You think, Tod?

Tod got up and pulled on his pants, then padded quietly
down the stairs. Halfway down he could hear that someone was
killing a piglet in the kitchen. It was the most peculiar sound –
definitely animal, a high-pitched squealing. There was a dying pig
in the kitchen. Then quiet again.

His mother was sitting on the floor at the sink end of the
kitchen. Her face was screwed up and bright red in effort. She
appeared to be sitting in a small puddle.

'Tod, thank God! Get an ambulance. Phone's on the side.
Can't get up. The baby's coming … '

Her words came out in peculiar little grunts and she started
squealing again, her face puce and unrecognisable. She actually
looked and sounded like a pig. Who knew childbirth did that? Tod
couldn't work out if she was trying to hold it in or push it out.

Her phone was lying by the kettle, true, but it was stone
dead. He punched the buttons harder, trying to make it work. Only
his mother could be nine months pregnant and forget to charge the
phone.

112

He rummaged frantically in his school bag but, of course, *shit!* – his phone was in his school locker!

The squealing stopped again, abruptly.

'Next time, I think, Tod, you'll, have, to help me. The baby's coming!' Little words jabbed out.

No – anything but that!

Let me take over.

How?

There's a switch.

A switch in my head?

Yes – look!

And Ed showed it to him.

You have to flip it.

Has that been there all the time?

No, I just found it. Neat, huh?

Ed – if I flip it, how does it get flipped back?

I have to do that.

How do I know you'll do it?

You trust me.

Tod really didn't trust him. In fact, if he had to bet his GCSEs on it, he would say that Ed would *definitely, positively, not in a million years* flip that switch back.

You promise, you'll do it?

Of course. What do you take me for?

A ruthless old git.

Ed thought as little as he could out loud. This was his chance. No way would he flip it back. He tried to send waves of love and trust to Tod.

Go on boy – do it! Maybe a little push ...

Tod, you had better get her undressed. It's only in Australian soap operas that women give birth with their knickers on. Open the front door and leave it wide. Get some clean towels and get some of them under her. Wash your hands thoroughly, right up to the elbows.

Have you done this before?

Hundreds of times in the Peace Corps. Oh and scissors and some shoe strings.

Tod tried to imagine what on earth Ed needed that lot for. He considered what he knew of childbirth. That took all of a nanosecond. He knew more about quantum physics or the creation of the universe. God, he knew more about *girls*.

Surely they had studied this at some point at school. He checked through his long-term memory. Nope. Hitler, atoms, quadratic equations, the Moslem way of life. No childbirth tucked in there anywhere. Either they hadn't done childbirth or he'd been away. His own mum needed help undressing – he muttered a short prayer and flipped the switch.

Yes! Yes! Yes! Hallo new body! Hallo new life!

Ed did a little shimmy of triumph round the kitchen. He noticed that his new hips worked perfectly. His old ones had been completely rubbish. Nice moves!

Mrs Mortimer was, however, in extreme distress and understandably getting very annoyed at her son prancing around the kitchen while she was in agony.

Ed's ancient Peace Corps training kicked in. He worked quickly, gathering fresh towels from the linen cupboard, putting the kettle on, taking a quick peek out of the front door but, (wouldn't you know it?) nobody there in the whole bloomin' street.

The cornering and acceleration on this new body was terrific. He skidded a bit across the kitchen just for fun, just missing the edges of the growing puddle. Now, reassure the patient.

'Don't worry, er ... mum, we can do this. We did it in Biology. Looked easy. Piece of cake-erooni!'

Funny, she still didn't look all that confident. *She* must have done it before, surely. What a fuss these women make. It was what God had created them for and they always did all this screaming and groaning.

Ed tried to persuade her to roll on her side so that he could get the towels underneath her, and was surprised to find she was much stronger than he. Moving twelve stone of Mrs M with Tod's sixteen-year-old body was surprisingly difficult.

He heaved, but nothing much happened. Her frequent cries of 'Geddoff!', 'Tod, b***** off!' and 'Get an adult!' were starting to really annoy him.

A quick trip to the downstairs loo to wash up, where due to Mrs M's paranoia about 'flu-related diseases there were loads of anti-bacterial wipes.

Another quick trip to the front door to inspect the totally deserted street – it could have been a lunar landscape. All that was out there was a lot of cold wet air and grey. Tumbleweed was blowing down the middle of the road.

Back in the kitchen and Mrs Mortimer looked terrified, sat sweating on her brightly coloured throne of beach towels. She looked as if all she needed was a bucket and spade. In the end though, it was two pushes and a scream from the mother (which must surely have attracted elephants in Africa) and the little girl was wrapped up in a SpongeBob Squarepants beach towel. Three pushes and the bundle included the afterbirth as well. Ed had pretty much nothing to do except catch. He tried to check the baby's airways, but she was yelling to beat the band, so he sort of guessed they were clear.

'Now listen, Tod, before everyone gets here. I need to talk to you. Sit down here. We need a serious talk, a heart-to-heart.'

'Now – are you sure? Shall I just make a nice cup of tea? You guys should maybe bond a bit? Have a cuddle?'

Ed's feeling of satisfaction ebbed away a fair bit. Tod was not going to exist, love. It was a shame, but in the words of the great sketch he was deceased, an ex-Tod.

Ed really didn't want a cosy chat with Tod's mum. Odds on, in fact racing cert, she was still fond of the lad. In fact, Ed quite liked him, although he found him a bit dim, a bit boring and too easily worked up over things.

Dismally, Ed sat down in the damp and tried to look like Tod – a bit gormless, a bit vacant but essentially *nice*.

Tod's mother had tears in her eyes. She held her new daughter to her and rocked her gently. The little girl stared up unblinkingly. Ed had a horrible feeling that she knew more than she was letting on. She didn't blink. Not once. There was something alien-like in her unwavering stare. Mrs M sniffed alarmingly and the tears started to roll down her cheeks.

'I've stuffed things up. You don't need to know any details, but lately I've really stuffed things up. I had a bad start in life, Tod, and I thought marrying your dad would sort it all out, but I just got so very, very bored. I made some bad decisions because I was, well, pretty well bored rigid and, well, you don't know what you have until you lose it.

'But I'm going to turn it around, I honestly mean it. Perhaps he will even come back to us. I'm going to be the best mum in the world to you and little Tracey.'

Tod certainly hadn't known what he had, and as far as Ed was concerned, you snooze, you lose, mate: use it or lose it! You could have chosen to catch the kid, but you chickened out. Lose-*ser!* Ed was trying to persuade himself that he felt OK about the body snatch, but he was starting to feel pretty bad about it. Perhaps he would get used to it.

'But you, I know you are the only thing in my life I've done right. This morning's proved that. You've got to try hard for me – stop this messing around at school – look after your little sister. You're my life, Tod, you know I love you to bits. Promise me, honey?'

Thank God! There was shouting down the hall and Lacey burst into the kitchen, which now looked like an amateur dramatics production of The Texas Chainsaw Massacre.

Lacey did a lot of girlie squealing.

'Wow, Mrs M! Are you OK? Are you OK? Oh my God! She looks just like Tod!'

Ed suspected the baby looked just like a certain ceramics lecturer.

Lacey, of course, could produce a charged-up mobile, on which she immediately called an ambulance. Tod was dispatched by both women to 'go and get some clothes on, for Heavens' sake, what are you like, look at you!'

The day seemed to go by in a blur from there.

A baby is like a seed. It lies there, tiny, looking up at you with unblinking eyes or sleeping with a bubble of milk in its mouth. But it is a start that might grow into anything. It is the first of many possibilities. When a baby is born, it shifts reality, for everyone.

Shane McCormick, ambulance driver, trained medic and film star in waiting, was told in breathless detail by the woman in the ratty pink candlewick dressing gown how her son had delivered her baby because 'he had learned how to do it in Biology'.

Her son standing nearby looked as if he couldn't deliver a pint of milk without dropping it. Mr McCormick agreed that it was 'marvellous what they learned in school', but his mind was on the words to the Christmas pantomime that he was learning for the local Puppet Players: a cross between Dick Whittington and Britain's Got Talent, with different young people auditioning for the part of a 'fun' Mayor of London. Shane was to play the part of Simon Powell, the main villain.

He needn't have bothered because he was to catch swine 'flu over Christmas and miss all the productions. He was understudied by his rival, who was spotted by a talent scout and went on to have a small but regular part in Coronation Street. All from yelling, 'He's behind you' in a particularly convincing manner. Shane became very bitter over it at one point, but he had a sunny disposition and got over it eventually.

Today, however, Shane noticed that the boy looked sick and miserable. He hoped he wasn't going to pass out, and gave him a stick of Kit Kat. The kid gave him a sheepish sort of grin. Shane thought he liked kids   if he didn't drive an ambulance, he would have liked to be a teacher. Perhaps he might go back to college if his film career didn't take off.

Lacey was so proud of Tod she could have exploded. She secretly texted her friend at the Chron and Ec (Chronicle and Echo – duh!) and told her about it. She had known he had potential.

Tod should lighten up a bit though. It was all over now and they were having a ride in the ambulance and a day off school. Maybe even a bit of time alone in an empty house. The ambulance lady had cleaned the kitchen up a bit and the bloke had given them Kit Kat.

Lacey decided never to have a baby. It looked gross.

Lorna Jones, ace reporter, texted back excitedly. When could she interview Tod? Could she bring a photographer? Was he Lacey's boyfriend?

Yes, yes, yes!

Jade and Jodie were leaning dangerously over the Year 11 balcony, because they knew it wound up the teacher on duty three floors down.

Could they get away with dropping a sweet wrapper? Maybe just a couple.

They let one drift down as an experiment and it drifted down like a little petal and landed at the teacher's feet.

Jade: 'I don't like Emos because they talk too fast.'

Jade talked pretty fast herself. Even Jodie sometimes had difficulty keeping up with her.

'They're alright on Facebook. Got loads of friends, I have. Hundreds – trying to get it up to a thousand by Christmas. Takes me ages to keep my wall up to date and to comment and stuff.'

'Yeah, 'cos they're like typing then and also they say some pretty sick stuff. But I don't like the black.'

'No, I look manky in black – all washed up.'

'Out?'

'Too cold.'

'No, "washed out", not "up". Not a jellyfish are you?'

They both shrieked with laughter, causing a small flock of Year 7s to run, terrified.

'Anyway, can't wear it. And I don't hang out with them 'cos they're vain. They just wear that stuff and talk about themselves. My mum says they're depressing. My mum says life is for living, not moping around feeling sorry for yourself. "You're a long time dead", is what she says. They should get over themselves.'

'Oh look – she's looking up at us. Hallo, miss! What do you think she's saying?'

'I'll just lean over a bit and try to see – hold onto me in case I overbalance. No I can't tell, but she's waving her arms about. Anyway, that Tod Wossisname helped his mum have a baby.'

'He's not an Emo, is he? Look she's coming up!'

'No, he's a hero, but I remembered 'cos it sounds the same. I know because Lacey in 11 Mandela texted Amber and Amber texted Kyle and Kyle texted Jason and Jason texted Sue – Sue Smith not Sue Spender – and Sue texted Jenny Smith in 11 Rosa Parkes and Jenny's my cousin, so she texted me. He's going to be in the

Chron and Ec. He said he knew what to do because he'd studied it in Biology. He doesn't do Biology, does he? She's got to the Year 10 landing – let's go for a fag.'

'Only the boffs do Biology. Tod does Crime Scenes and shit with us. End of break really. Have we got time?'

'Yeh – we'll share.'

Shane watched Jade and Jodie stalk off across the Year 11 balcony towards the sixth form loos. They were goddesses. Tod was a hero.

Shane knew all about it because Sue (Smith not Spender) had told her brother Wayne and Wayne had texted Shane's cousin Wanda in 9LutherKing. Wow! Lacey was going to video Tod talking about it on her iPhone and put it up on YouTube. Tod was famous.

Shane sighed and felt sorry for himself. He was just a fat kid who none of the girls talked to. He stomped off to ICT, where he thought of a great social networking idea which eventually made him a millionaire.

In twenty years' time lots of girls talked to him. He didn't always talk to them, but it was great to have the choice.

Miss Hamilton reached the Year 11 balcony to find it deserted. She leaned, exhausted on the stairwell. Mr Foster smiled at her on the way past. It was the first time she had noticed him. It was the first time he had noticed her.

They stopped for a chat whilst their classes enacted a small riot, during which Sue Spender's glasses were broken and Tod's Maths book was thrown out of a third story window into the playground, where a large short-sighted seagull tried to eat it under the impression it was a sandwich.

Mrs Fiona Mortimer looks at the little baby in the baby tank next to her. Little scrunched-up face with big blue staring eyes over the pink hospital blanket and she just knows everything is going to be different from now on.

'Thank you, Tod,' she whispers, as he reluctantly bends down to take his leave.

'Do me a favour, then, er Mum. Gracie not Tracey. Would that be OK?'

'Alright, yes, that's nice.'

Outside the ward, Lacey throws her arms round Tod and kisses him.

'My brilliant boyfriend!'

This is just wrong,

Ed thinks.

Apart from the fact that I'm seventy, dead, and should not under any theory of any universe anywhere be kissing a sixteen-year-old girl, it's just wrong to kiss anyone after you've stopped breathing, especially someone else's bird.

Already I've stolen these memories. I'm going to steal an entire life, and in the end I'll just end up old again. There has to be a way out.

Think, Ed!

Nothing occurred to him. He was trapped.

Whopp! Whopp! Whopp! A proper photographer with a proper camera and a proper flash thingy takes photographs of Tod for the Chron and Ec.

, Lorna tries to get Tod to say something interesting, but she gives up and decides to make it all up as usual. She wonders if she can sell the story to one of the nationals? She is trying so hard to make contacts in London and kick-start her career.

She gets Tod to cuddle a completely empty beach towel, as if it is a baby. Ed looks out at her from Tod's face and tries a shy teenage smile. He needs to get the hang of this. He looks creepy.

Gracie sleeps tight, wrapped in her pink hospital blanket in the baby tank. She dreams of the womb and of milk. She has no schemes, no plans, just a future, and her birth has already shifted reality.

Ed lies on Tod's bed and looks up at the weird stain on the ceiling. He feels unaccountably sad and a bit guilty – and yes, very lonely.

His funeral is next week.

Oh well. Perhaps he can start enjoying life after that.

TWELVE

*In which Ed takes the advice
offered by a bunch of lilies.*

The experience of living someone else's life is not an easy one. You look at someone and think their life is easy, but in fact they struggle with stuff in the same way you do. The only difference is some people get depressed and bottle it up, and some people brave it out and they appear to be doing fine.

They're not though. Ed remembered a joke: before you criticise someone, walk a mile in their shoes – then you're a mile away from them and you have their shoes.

It was true, though. Tod's life wasn't easy. Everyone wanted him to do something he didn't want to do, but then when he was sure what he wanted to do, when he was playing football or with Lacey, it seemed everything came together to stop him doing it.

And that shoe shop was a bloomin' nightmare! Ed was sure he would kick that into touch. Who needed all those smelly feet? The cheese got onto his fingers – OK, Tod's fingers – no, *his* fingers and just wouldn't wear off.

Who knew the life of a teenage boy was so complicated?

'The tears of a clown' isn't just an expression, it's a fact. Everyone laughs when they're dying inside. Everybody struggles with stuff: getting on with people, concentrating, being woken up at three in the morning by a screaming baby, simultaneous equations, missing an open goal, saying the right thing to your 'girlfriend' (such as, 'Are you really my girlfriend – when did that happen? No, I'm sorry, I missed it.' And, 'No way am I having my hair cut like Justin Bieber,') and just generally stuff like that.

Ed was struggling. It seemed that everything he could do in his own life, he was still able to do. For example, he could read music, he knew all the words to the Beatles songs, could do all the GCSE Maths standing on his head (no call for that though), could dance like a hippy … and still he didn't understand women.

On the upside, he had been put up a set in Maths already (into Lacey's set).

There were three reasons for this.

Reason one: Ed was now the most mathematically able person (including the younger members of the Maths department) in the school, because he did his GCSEs and A Levels in the fifties, when men were men and Maths was Maths.

Reason two: the teacher in his usual set couldn't find Tod's Maths book and thought he might have left it down the pub.

Reason three: the teacher from his last Maths set couldn't wait to get rid of Tod.

Unfortunately, though, Ed couldn't do all the things Tod could do and which everybody expected. He couldn't ignore his mum and his teachers completely, or walk through the squalor in his bedroom without tidying up, and he kept falling off that bloomin' bike. His arse, or at least he supposed Tod's arse, was black and blue.

He couldn't text. He couldn't speak without the youngsters around him falling about laughing – and he didn't know why.

In addition to this, he also experienced a lot of weird emotion that was related to Tod's body. He had to ignore his mother and his teachers because he only had so much attention to give and that was devoted to Lacey. He needed to know where she was, who she was talking to. What she was talking about (was it *him*?) and if she was actually with him, that was disaster.

He was aware of everything about her: how she was sitting, how she laughed, he felt her breathe and he was aware of her thigh shifting on her chair. He loved her little overbite and the way her bag was packed with everything for the day in the order she needed it.

All of that was apparently linked to Tod's physical responses to Lacey and, for Ed, it was a pain. Ed was fed up with avoiding Lacey's attempts to 'cuddle' him. He was fed up with saying the wrong thing and people whispering about it behind his back. Well, Tod's back.

Ed didn't need to see the love in other people's eyes that was meant for Tod. He was well fed up with being a squatter.

So the day before his funeral, which after all was supposed

126

to be *his* big day, he was lying in Tod's room, in Tod's cramped single bed, under Tod's black duvet cover, worrying about Tod.

It was stupid. Tod could have walked under a bus and bought it. *This* was much kinder than that.

Everybody thought zombie Tod was the real Tod and everybody was happy. Well not Tod, obviously, but he wasn't *un*happy – he just *wasn't*.

Ed listened as the birds started to sing a bit. One of them appeared to have a bit of a cough. Probably an old pigeon, ready to fall off the branch. One day you're napping, then there's a cat and you're just a bundle of grey feathers being forced through the catflap. Life was cruel.

The grey light of dawn was creeping under Tod's black-on-black-with-a-hint-of-black bedroom curtains. What was it with teenagers and black? If you lived in a funeral home, you should expect Death to come knocking, right? Anything could have happened to Tod at any minute quite naturally. The boy wasn't exactly careful. You could have died from salmonella by just inhaling in his bedroom. He could have been knocked down in that fight and trampled to death. A toilet might have fallen on his head, like that girl in the series. Or a piano, like George Clooney in the ad. For hours, it seemed, Ed wrestled with what had happened and what he was supposed to do.

Was he avoiding Heaven or Hell? It would be Heaven, surely. He had saved a good few lives during his service in Malawi. Then, on the other hand, he had killed Marie and, he supposed, Tod.

Did it count if you killed people when you weren't looking? Wasn't that sort of 'collateral damage'? God must make some sort of allowance surely. Some sort of 'money off' deal. Or …

Ed drifted off into the delicious sleep that claims you half an hour before you have to get up anyway – that warm, happy sleep that cuddles you tight and feeds you chocolate.

Almost as soon as he was really warm and snuggly, Tod's mobile went off really loudly next to Tod's right ear.

'Tod – Tod – is that you?'

Best not to answer that honestly …

'It's Sophie from the nursing home! Tod, be an absolute lamb. I really need your help.'

Ed got ready to break in and say, 'No.' Not being 'an absolute lamb' was one of the life policies that had served him so well for so long. In his experience, women were not an eighth as helpless as they made out.

'I've got this old duck here for the funeral. Her family are all over, loads of them, but they said could she stay here because she's a bit doolally … you know, the wheel's going round but quite honestly the hamster's long gone. Nice old duck, but she's pushing me over the edge. Can you just come down and talk to her about Ed for a bit? She seems to have been very fond of him. She says it was hot when she knew him, so I guess it was in the Peace Corps. I've got the breakfasts to do and she won't leave me alone. It'll be twenty minutes tops – just before school.'

'Yeah, OK.'

At least this was someone for him and not Tod, and presumably someone who was sorry to see him go. Perhaps it was one of the nurses from the hospital, heartbroken at his passing.

Mrs M was feeding Gracie in the kitchen so Ed, still feeling pretty stupid in school uniform, shouted out where he was going. Averting his eyes in a gentlemanly manner, he fell over his own shoes on his way out of the kitchen, stumbled into the umbrella stand, slammed the front door and fell off the bike a record three times on his way to the nursing home. So he wasn't in the best of moods when he got there.

Then he had to text Lacey that he was going to meet her at school and predictably (what was it with her?) she'd phoned him straight back to tell him to remember his games kit. That was OK because he hadn't remembered to take it home for washing in the first place – or Tod hadn't.

It was confusing and it gave him a headache.

Sophie was uncharacteristically flustered. 'She's a dear, really. She's been here since Friday. The whole family came over. She was OK when her daughter and grandson were here to pop in, but they've gone on a trip to Camden today to see yet more family and all she will say is, "When is Ed coming?" or "Ed is coming, when will he be here?" It breaks your heart. Big tears in her eyes, as well. I tried telling her Ed was dead, but all she will say is, "He's not gone yet." Please, Tod, just talk to her for a bit try to to get through. Her name is Marie, Marie O'Connell.'

'No!' Ed backed off. She was alive! Well, probably not for that much longer, but still. He felt too ashamed to see her. Still, she wouldn't know it was him, would she?

'No, I can't!'

'She's a very distressed old lady. Apparently she's been confused for a while now. She's been ill and she's still not at all well. Come on, Tod, it's really not like you to make a fuss. Where's the famous lad who takes delivering babies in his stride?'

One baby, Ed thought, *and he hadn't so much delivered it as got out of the stork's way. No, it wasn't like Tod. That's because it wasn't Tod.*

Still, Ed knew he couldn't walk away from what was left of Ed World to go and attend registration in Tod World. He could see her one more time and say goodbye.

Marie wasn't in Sophie's little office, though. Instead there was a little old lady with thin strands of white hair sticking up all over her pink head and rounded shoulders. She wore a polyester dress and thick, old-lady stockings.

Ed's heart sank. Then she turned towards him and he saw Marie's eyes and heard her soft Irish voice.

'It's about time, Ed, you eejit. I've been waiting here for days. That gobshite Michael has buggered off to see the cousins, thank the Lord! Mother of God, man, what are you wearing?'

'Marie, Marie ... '

Ed was choked. She was so *old* and crinkly. 'Can you see me?'

'Of course I can see you. Though it's no great treat I can tell you. I've messages to give you from all the flowers.'

'I loved you.'

'I loved you with all my heart and all my soul. It wasn't my heart and soul that got into trouble though, was it? A lot of good it did me, a sweet young Irish girl coming home from London, three months pregnant, no father for the babe and no husband for a wedding. Scared stiff and up the pole. It nearly killed my old lady but, fair play to her, she looked after me and the babe. You didn't love me half as much as you loved yourself.'

It was the moment – the moment to say he was wrong, that he had treated her badly and that he was sorry.

'It was a long time ago, it's true. Still, I do hope the devil catches up with my cousin Michael, for his part in it. Preferably not when he's flying the auld Ryanair with me, though!'

Her claw-like hands gripped her walking stick and she tried to get up. As he went to help, like lightning her wrinkled hands reached out and clutched his young ones.

'And whose clothes are you wearing? They're still not your own. Still living another man's life, Ed? Let me tell you what the flowers said. I've come all this way at my age to give you the messages and you will listen.'

'Flowers? Come on, flowers are talking to you? When flowers start talking to you, you are losing it. You can't go listening to flowers.'

Marie ignored him.

'I've remembered it all this time. The big golden chrysanthemum – we sell a lot of those because they're a nice cemetery flower – said to tell you not to steal if you could not live with your theft. The red roses say your love will follow you soon. I'm telling you it won't be that soon, so don't hold your breath, so to speak. Those roses are a bit soppy – you should hear how they go on on Valentine's Day. Neither will I be having anything to do with you if you go to The Other Place, which I see as a distinct possibility. I like the blue cornflowers because they remind me of summer. They said to tell you that summer is over and the pale lilies – you know those waxy ones you can spray with glitter – mind you they hate it – say winter is the time to turn to the darkness and rest.'

'You talk to the flowers?'

'No, man, they talk to me. I'm not bonkers! You need to give those clothes back and go with dignity.'

Ed couldn't cope with this. He could only just glimpse his lovely girl trapped inside the old-lady body, peeping out at him, playing hide and seek. He suddenly had to get out and he bent down to her and gently dropped a kiss onto her wrinkled mouth.

'You said it was hot where you knew me.'

'We were hot.'

Suddenly he was holding a young girl. Her eyes twinkled and her slight body clung to his. Their lips met and it was fifty years ago.

'Goodbye, Marie.'

'See you around, Ed.'

He wheeled the hated bike slowly home. He would tell Mrs M he felt ill and he'd sleep a bit longer.

It was a great day. The air was cold but the sun was shining. The sky had Simpson clouds scudding across it and the birds were singing full-pelt now. The leaves had turned and you could smell winter in the air. Soon the leaves would start to fall. When Grace got a bit older they could do leaf prints, like when he was little.

He remembered the smell of the green, red, yellow and blue poster paints and the dirty water standing in jam jars in the classroom. He wanted one more Christmas – to see a Christmas tree again with little chocolate snowmen on it, like when he was a kid. He had been allowed to turn the bakelite tree lights off every evening: a blue snowman, Father Christmas heads, green, orange and pink Chinese lanterns.

Ed filled his lungs and felt the cold, clean air like chilled wine in his throat. He had the whole of Tod's life ahead of him and he wanted it so badly it hurt him. He wanted to play football and eat food with real taste.

Next year he would be in the sixth form and then uni. He wanted to study and to meet pretty girls. Maybe he even wanted a family of his own, to watch them grow up – for them to know him.

Why should he give it back? Just because some bonkers old biddy brought him a message from a bunch of flowers?

Another deep, clean breath – so good, so cold.

He bought an ice-cream from the newsagents at the school gates, from an Asian gentleman who growled, 'Shouldn't you be in school?'

'Dentist.'

'Ice-cream after the dentist?'

'Check up.'

He wheeled the bike back into the park and sat on a bench to eat the ice-cream, which was already running down his wrist onto the sleeve of his school shirt. The sweet goo tasted wonderful.

There were some late pansies in the flower bed near the bench. They disapproved of him, but they ignored him and he ignored them. A couple of pigeons landed hopefully next to him, but flew away when he offered them nothing.

He should really get up and go home, or get up and go to school.

He sat, head back, staring at the blue sky, and started to cry.

Mrs Hardcastle, on her way to the dentist for three fillings looked at the young lad sitting on the park bench, sobbing his heart out.

'They're all on bloody drugs,' she muttered.

Ed flipped the switch.

THIRTEEN

In which the funeral is disrupted
by someone dying.

7.08

Tod was lying in Tod's room, in Tod's cramped single bed under Tod's black duvet cover, worrying about Ed. Ed was still asleep and it had to be about seven because the light was just creeping under the black curtain line. One of the pigeons out there had a hell of a cough. It was probably on the Woodbines! Get it: a woodpigeon on Woodbines!

Tod should really be using this Ed-free part of the day for a bit of 'me-time', but honestly, Ed was obviously having a bit of a crisis, even for a dead guy. He'd seemed really sorry about not flipping the switch back and Tod didn't really understand why.

It hadn't been like years. Tod had actually missed a Cheesy Feet Saturday and a Maths test. He had also gone up to the top Maths set, where he could sit next to Lacey. If he knew her, and he was beginning to know her very well indeed, all his work would be checked and corrected and generally approved before it ever hit the teacher's desk: *result*.

Also, Marie was alive and kicking. Tod smiled as an image of a karate kicking granny strolled across his mind. *'Karate Kid' starring Jackie Nan!*

Still, it must be a bit gross to really go to your own funeral. It might even be a bit scary. It sort of brought home to you that you really were dead.

Lacey had been round yesterday and had sorted him out with her dad's black tie, and she was going to the service with him. Ed knew how to tie a tie of course, so that was alright.

What could possibly go wrong?

Tod's mum sat breastfeeding her tiny daughter, watching her eyes droop shut as she filled up on milk, a little bubble forming at the corner of her mouth as she reached overflowing point.

She laid her tenderly in her cot, careful not to disturb her. As she tiptoed back to her own room, Gracie let loose a huge and resounding burp and woke herself up. She thought for a minute, before she decided she could fit in just a little more milk and gave a heart-rending wail.

Mrs Mortimer settled back down, nursing the baby and listening to the pigeons coughing outside the window. Gracie felt uncomfortably full and decided to push a little out into her nappy. Actually, that felt quite unpleasant. Time to cry.

8.05

The pigeons and Gracie went back to sleep. Everybody else had to get up. Gracie slept, happy and snuggled in her Moses basket, whilst her mother drank coffee in the kitchen, feeling like she had sand under her eyelids.

Down the hill in the nursing home, Sophie was facing the challenge of getting Marie and three other senior citizens ready for Ed's funeral. They had drafted more staff in, but it was still a bit of a rush.

Marie was a dear but obviously a bit ga-ga. She kept forgetting Ed was dead at all and actually asked if he were going to be at the funeral! Then apparently the pot plant in the dining room told her to put on some lipstick.

The rather elaborate arrangements for the whole affair (no ice swans, thank God, but still loads of exact instructions) had been passed on to the vicar and, bless him, Ed had sourced all the music and readings and everything himself.

What could go wrong?

Mr Worthington forgot he had put his bacon sandwich on his chair and sat on it. In the resulting confusion the plump little care worker knocked over a full mug of tea into Mrs Dawkins' lap. Mrs Dawkins called her 'a great lummox' and she burst into tears and went and shut herself in the laundry room.

Sophie sighed and started the clean up. It was like some bizarre game show.

9.30

Ed and Tod strolled through the park. They were passing time before the service.

> Bloomin' cold.

> *Yeh, well, it's like nearly winter.*

> These are our school trousers.

> *I don't go to a lot of funerals. Only my nan's.*

> The leaves are beautiful as they start to turn.

> *Leaves? What are you on about?*

> Look about you – the whole park's beautiful. The flowers, the trees, the kiddies.

> *There's no kiddies – they're all at school and they're like snotty screaming urban terrorists when they are here. It's just a rather manky park. Wanna get an ice-cream?*

> Vanilla.

> *Chocolate.*

> Vanilla.

> *Chocolate.*

> Vanilla and chocolate.

> *I'm a teenager – I get my own way.*

> I'm old – show some respect.

> *I'll outlive you.*

> Good luck with that, son.

10.30

The crowd outside the chapel was amazing. Sophie had contacted people, but it looked like those people had contacted people and those people had contacted people and it was just a huge crowd of old people, jostling each other for the best position, laughing, catching up, messing up the gravel. There was very little black, either, Tod noticed. Well, black clothing; there were loads of black people, including one sizeable lady of advancing years who appeared to be wearing a huge red and orange tent.

Tod tried to guess who were the aging pop stars, but everyone seemed to be in there with a chance.

Sophie and a little care worker turned up in the home's minibus with no less than three wrinklies. They had managed to capture two in wheelchairs, but Sophie still looked stressed. Her hair was coming out of its bun in great strands and she kept pinning it back in place. For some reason one of her old people, a sweet looking little old lady in a wheelchair, was clutching a spider plant in a pot. She appeared to be talking to it.

Lacey had taken the opportunity to go full Goth, with black lace veil and long black gloves.

She looks fit.

She looks like Morticia bloomin' Addams.

10.45

The chapel was nice, Tod and Ed agreed. They were finally all seated, although there had been some nasty moments whilst the oldies fought for seats with whatever weapons were available (mostly selective deafness, walking sticks and Zimmer frames). The wheelchairs blocked the centre bit.

There was an unexpected bit of sun which shone through the stained glass and caused red, green and blue shadows to chase around the chapel. Ed had gone very quiet at the sight of the coffin but was now chattering away again, making Tod crane round to see who was there.

That's a bloke I worked with in Malawi and his wife. I think he married a nurse. He certainly knew a lot of nurses if you know what I mean. There's the bloke from the betting shop. I think he's a consultant at the General – I used to do some orderly work there. There's Mick and Marie. My God, the drummer's wearing a hearing aid. Dave's wearing a purple velvet suit. Poser. That's a bloke I used to write with on NME and that's that bank nurse from Muswell Hill. They all look so old!

At least they're alive – that's one up on you. What do you mean, Marie? I thought she fell tragically to her death off Suicide Bridge in the sixties? Why is she waving at me?

Long story. There's that bird who used to cook me paella on the beach. Look, and my dentist. Nice to see Jim's escaped the Sunset for a day.

10.50

The vicar looked round the packed Chapel. This man was certainly well liked, even if his friends were a bit unusual. The woman in orange with purple hair and a little dog in her handbag started to eat a sandwich. More than a little unusual. The dog was given the remnants of the sandwich.

'Dearly beloved, we are here today to celebrate the life of Edward Frederick Montgomery Fisher ... '

'And they're off,' the bookmaker in the pew behind said loudly.

Gracie dozed as Mrs M jiggled her and encouraged her heavy eyelids to close. The little white milk spots dappled her plump cheeks. Tod's father sidled in at the back of the chapel to keep an eye on the boy. Mick O'Connell bent down to Marie, pretending he was checking on her but really looking for the Werther's Originals she usually hid down the side of her wheelchair. She was sound asleep.

'And Edward requested that this piece of music be played for the special lady in his life.' The tinkly introduction to the Stones' 'She's a Rainbow' rang out in the Chapel and at least six old ladies started sobbing uncontrollably, obviously under the impression that it was for them.

A rainbow crossed Marie's face from the sun shining through the stained glass. She smiled and got up.

Tod and Ed saw a young girl get up from the wheelchair and walk towards them. She smiled, and to Ed it was the most beautiful smile in the universe.

As she reached them, she held out both hands.

Come on Ed, it's time to go. It seems the roses were right.

I don't know how, Marie, I can't get out! I'm stuck!

Tod could feel Ed frantically struggling in his head. He couldn't find a way out. The pain was terrible. Tod roared, clutching his head. He staggered into the aisle and sank to his knees, groaning. As the music came to a stop, everyone turned to watch him. He was writhing on the floor of the chapel, his eyes turned up to show only the whites, spit foaming from his mouth.

'Get him out! Stop it! Ed!'

He was screaming and screaming, and then he curled up into a little ball and sobbed. Ed tried to think: how could he get out? Why was he stuck in the first place? Where was the switch for this one?

The sun went in and the little chapel was suddenly dark.

Shadows crept in from the sides of the walls. Just the sound of Tod groaning and a pulse beating in their head.

I can't get out!

Tod could sort of feel Ed struggling in his brain. It was like the bit that was Ed had roots and the roots had tiny roots and those tiny roots stretched deep into the bit that was Tod.

The pain was terrible as the smallest parts of the roots started to pull out. Tod could see it all clearly, not with his eyes, but sort of behind his eyes. It was as if huge tree roots were stretching deep into his very thoughts. There were so many little rootlets – he couldn't see how he was ever going to be Tod again and how Ed was ever going to be Ed.

He had the sensation that some of the little roots were just snapping off. Perhaps a part of him was always going to be Ed. Perhaps it was too late now for Ed to leave. He did not know it, but his groaning had risen almost to a scream, a weird high-pitched, wailing noise.

Then he felt Ed relax again and the pull stopped. A deep, inky sadness spread through his head, like a stain.

I'm sorry, Marie, I can't get out.

She smiled.

There was I thinking you were apologising for what you did.

I am sorry, truly sorry. I do want to come with you now.

I forgive you.

Then Ed was free – just like that. Tod felt the little roots almost shrink back into the part of his brain that was Ed, as if they were dying.

Ed sprang upwards. In one leap Ed was free and young, and he took Marie in his arms and held her. It seemed to him that he could feel her and that all was right with the universe.

The pain stopped and Tod became aware of a number of things.

He was lying on the floor of the chapel and a lot of people were looking at him. Lacey was kneeling at his side, apparently trying to force a pink plastic hairbrush into his mouth.

It was very quiet indeed. He realised that this was because he had stopped screaming.

The middle part of his body was very cold indeed, because there were two ghosts standing in it, snogging each other.

Hey, guys, get a room! You're standing in my ... well ... in me.

The ghosts stepped quickly to one side. Tod could see them quite clearly, but then when he thought about it, he couldn't see them at all. He could see peace and happiness (two characteristics which he had not associated with Ed lately) and he felt they were golden, or silver ... or somehow sparkly.

I think I'm leaving now. Tod, Listen to a dead guy: try to stay out of trouble, do your homework, look after your Mum, say 'no' to drugs and always wear a condom.

All at the same time?

Smartarse!

Don't go, Ed!

Really?

No – go! Erm, take care!

Ed made an awkward little gesture of farewell, and he and Marie walked up the aisle together.

There was a little argument at the coffin when Ed obviously

wanted to have a bit of a look inside, and then they stood together at the altar rail, just as at a wedding, holding ghostly hands, and slowly faded from Tod's view.

Tod's head felt empty. It was like when his mum had decided to chuck away the really big settee from the lounge and hadn't bought a replacement for weeks. There was a sense that it used to be a lot more crowded in Tod's head and it would take a bit of getting used to. It felt just a bit lonely, too.

It was at this point that it was discovered that the old lady in the wheelchair was not just snoozing through the funeral ceremony, but had in fact joined Ed in eternal rest. The fuss and bother did at least stop Lacey ramming the plastic handle of the hairbrush into his mouth before she damaged his teeth (apparently under the impression that Tod was having some sort of epileptic fit and might swallow his own tongue).

It turned into a nightmare for the vicar. Funerals are timed very exactly at chapels of rest. You book a slot. It was like when you went ten pin bowling. When you had finished your game, the next guys got the lane and they didn't expect you to slope off and have a burger in the middle so that they were kept waiting. The cheery ambulance drivers had arrived and, in concerned but still very loud voices, confirmed that Marie was, in fact, dead.

Shane McCormick, ambulance driver and star-in-waiting, even took a look at Tod while he was there and said that he ought to see a GP because he might have had a fit.

'Told you so!' Lacey said triumphantly.

They took Marie's chair (and Marie, of course) out to the

ambulance through the by now thoroughly overexcited crowd. The vicar had to finish the ceremony in record time. He gabbled through the story of Ed's life and a couple of prayers, like a recorder on fast forward.

Nobody listened.

There was a baby screaming flat out and the dog started howling in competition. A man in the fifth row started to pass sweets amongst the pews. The boy who had apparently had a fit was having a loud argument with his Goth girlfriend about what you do if someone has a fit.

In the back row a group of older guys passed around a cigarette, apparently under the impression they were invisible. Nobody really noticed when the coffin slid away on its final journey and Ed went to eternal peace, surrounded by the living shouting at each other.

The end music was 'I hope I die before I get old', which Reverend Hargreaves thought was most inappropriate.

It was a most unusual funeral. The vicar had to go and have a lie down afterwards, which was a shame because he missed the fireworks display outside.

FOURTEEN

*In which Tod finds the meaning of life
and a very smelly baby.*

'So what have you learned?'

They were reviewing Tod's Pastoral Support Programme. His mum was sitting opposite him, with Grace gurgling and smelling quite spectacularly unpleasant, Tod noticed, in one of those baby basket things at her feet.

Brown nappy time, he thought.

His dad was also there. How did that happen? His dad seemed to be about all the time now, taking Grace out, moaning on about Tod's homework and Tod staying out late.

The Head of Year had asked the question and was now

poised, pen in hand, ready to write down whatever Tod said, provided he got a move on and said something before she got fed up and answered it for him.

Tod knew it was going to be all right because they were actually pleased with him for once. He had delivered a baby and gone up a Maths set. Neither of those deeds was actually Tod, but he was willing to take the credit.

Grace took the pressure off by making a resounding squelchy farting noise and Tod thought quickly. It was either that or suffocate. He knew from experience that Grace would only be happy for a couple of minutes before the warm stuff in her nappy became cold and then she would treat them to her siren scream to alert them that Her Majesty would like her nappy changed.

What had he learned?

- Chlamydia is a disease, not a posh baby name (and incidentally having sex has its own hazards).
- More than one person per head is too crowded.
- You should do the brackets first.
- Some gorgeous women dressed as police officers are actually police officers.
- Adults stuff things up just as much as teenagers (possibly moreso, because they have more stuff to deal with).
- Don't gamble something you don't want to lose. For example, if someone says, 'you can trust me with your life', you probably should think very hard before you tell them where to go.
- Lacey would slap him if he tried to do more

147

than kiss her (this was a very recent discovery and Tod hoped this could be changed pretty soon by patience and agreeing with her a lot).

- Babies smell.
- Changing a nappy is not as easy as it looks on the adverts because
  a) babies hide an awful lot in their nappies
  b) they don't stay still and smile and make little gurgling noises, like they do on the ads
  c) if you get even a tiny bit of cream on your fingers, the sticky bit won't stick
  d) you always put something you need just out of reach and then have to carry the baby over to it and she then takes the opportunity to wee down your best T-shirt
  e) stuff gets under your fingernails
  f) your mobile phone always goes in the middle and it's always someone trying to sell you a better mobile phone.
- Life goes by very quickly and you should decide things for yourself because it's your life, not theirs.
- He never wanted to run a shoeshop.
- Someone had found his Maths book in the middle of the tennis court.
- The boys who ran the Christian Union and the Origami Club were cool.

- If a ghost stands inside you, you feel very cold indeed.

None of those things seemed like the sort of thing she was wanting.

'Dunno really,' he said, and she sighed in an exaggerated manner and suggested he had learned to 'get his head down' and 'take himself more seriously.'

'Yeah,' Tod agreed. 'That's OK.'

'So what do you want out of life, Tod?' Couldn't she smell Grace? What was wrong with her nose? You could practically cut a slice of that smell and hand it round on a plate. What was she thinking?

'Fresh air,' Tod said pointedly.

After that Grace opened up with her best point nine yell and they all agreed the PSP was finished, the meeting was over and Tod was generally cured and better in every way.

Tod's mum changed Grace in the visitors' toilets and came out with most of the poo over her own clothes.

Tod and his dad went to Mcdonald's.

They sat in companiable silence stuffing Big Macs and fries. Tod noticed his dad had a diet coke. He was eating enough calories to feed the whole of America for the day and drinking diet coke. Tod would never understand adults.

'So,' his dad said, 'what do you want out of life?'

'What do *you* want?' Tod asked.

'I guess, just to be happy.'

'And are you?'

'What?'

'Happy. Are you happy?'

'No, Tod, no I'm not.'

Silence fell as they both ate really fast to try to get the last chips.

'More chips?'

'Yeah.'

Sort yourself out, Tod thought angrily. *If you want what you've got, fine. If you want to come back to Mum, fine. Neither is going to be perfect because nothing ever is. I'm not going to tell you what to do – I've had enough of being tangled up in someone else's life to last me my own lifetime. I've spent the last few weeks with a dead guy in my head.*

What do I want? To live every minute! More fries!

EPILOGUE

A baby changes things. They are magic. Their influence spreads out and seeps into those around them.

Similarly, those who are near the end of life change things. They exert a power.

Nobody more ordinary than Ed and Grace.

Nobody more powerful than Ed and Grace.

Kevin Turner stayed on for the sixth form, went to Leicester Uni and became a PE teacher. He and Tod never spoke again, despite being in many of the same classes. And Kevin stayed well away from Lacey (which was good because it meant she didn't have to hurt him again – she had slightly bruised the side of her foot last time).

Mr Jones, the Maths teacher, quit his job, left his wife and became an alpaca farmer in Yorkshire. The alpacas loved him and smiled at him with their long woolly faces every morning. He did his own accounts and became steadily richer.

His wife eventually got married again – to another Maths teacher.

Some people never learn.

Jade became a civil rights lawyer and Jodie became an MP. They wore sharp little business suits and carried expensive briefcases. Their brains were sharp and cut through arguments like knives. When they clicked their way into court and the Houses of Commons respectively, balanced on their tiny little cost-a-heels shoes, men were terrified of them. They sat in sharp London bars and drank chilled white wine, watching people and laughing quietly together.

They still took 'no crap from nobody' – probably even less.

Shane McCormick, ambulance driver, missed his big chance to be in Coronation Street and sank into a deep depression as he realised fame and fortune had passed him by. He spent weeks dressed in stripy pyjamas on the sofa, watching daytime television and eating cheesy wotsits.

He came to three realisations. First, he realised that daytime television is rubbish. Second, he realised that there are only so many days you can wear stripy pyjamas without washing them before you start to hate yourself. Third, he realised that he was in the wrong job. He saw clearly that he was really good at communicating with teenagers and that he would make a great secondary school teacher.

He was wrong. And wrong.

Shame.

The Assistant Head of Year quit her job and became an ambulance worker, because she thought she would be good at it. She was good at it but it did her back in. She didn't mind.

Tod's dad spent so much time at Tod's mum's house that That Slapper realised their relationship was going nowhere and dumped him. Tod thought it was funny (so did Tod's mum).

His dad started to spend a lot of time round Tod's house in the evenings, until it eventually became his house again.

Grace drank and ate, snoozed and filled her nappy. She loved the three faces she saw all the time. Tod was her favourite. He did a stupid voice for her and pulled faces. She had a sunny nature and laughed at him until she hiccoughed in her baby walker, jerking it all over the kitchen floor.

Tod went back to volunteering at the nursing home after school and sometimes Lacey helped him. He stopped the Saturday job and offered to work Saturdays at the home for pay. Sophie was happy to agree. Tod said life was too short to sell shoes.

It gave Sophie some afternoons off and it gave Tod a sense of calm. It gave Lacey lots more people to boss around (at least, those who couldn't move fast enough to get away from her).

Despite having a lot more people in his life, Tod felt lonely at times. They were all alive, and he was used to having the undead for company.

He often went down to Ed's grave and stood there quietly. It was nice there, just people caring for the graves, loads of flowers, birdsong and an open sky. Sometimes he took a book down there.

Lacey said it was 'dead weird', but she came along sometimes. Other times, he would go alone, just to get away from people.

He would stand still and listen for Ed, but he was never there.

Still, Tod always went away feeling happy.

RAVEN

Some other great reads
from Raven Books …

Taken
Rosemary Hayes

Losing your dad may not be the hardest thing.

Four years ago, Kelly's dad disappeared, apparently having taken his own life. His family are left devastated and are only just beginning to move on.

Then, one day, Kelly thinks she sees him again. It is enough to bring back all the painful memories. Why did he kill himself? What was so terrible that he couldn't go on? The thoughts won't leave her alone.

Kelly confides in her friend Jack, and as they try to find out more about Dad's past they unearth a confusing mass of inconsistencies and unanswered questions. Gradually they are sucked into a murky world where nothing is as it seems.

" ... a well-constructed story told by a very experienced author who knows just when – and how – to increase the tension."

Pauline Francis, awfullybigreviews.blogspot.com

ISBN 978-178591-358-7
£7.99

A Brightness
out of the Blue
Jill Atkins

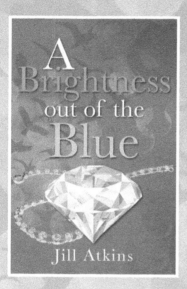

When you're at rock bottom …
life can't get any worse …
you don't see the point of carrying
on …
someone walks into your world
and makes all the difference.

Ella is mourning her dead mother and suffering the cruelty of a new step-mother. But when Martha, an old lady, falls in the street and Ella helps her get home, she feels Martha's strange magical power. Soon her life begins to change for the better.

A Brightness out of the Blue is a beautiful modern-day fairytale with a twist in the tale.

ISBN 978-178591-350-1
£7.99

The Stone Balancer
John Townsend

Fin's fourteenth summer, at home by the sea in August, should be fantastic … but it isn't.

He's a keen stone-balancer, spending hours alone on the beach building stone towers. That's where he is the only witness to an apparent murderer on the cliff.

There's no body and there's no evidence of murder, but Fin is convinced that somebody has been killed. With his mother seriously ill and a nasty uncle now in charge, Fin is pursued and forced into hiding.

"A first-class read, full of adventure and ultimate hope – a real page-turner! A remarkable murder mystery with all sorts of ramifications. Not for the overly sensitive or vulnerable. I particularly liked the ending … Great stuff!"
Healthy Books www.healthybooks.org.uk

ISBN 978-178591-362-4
£7.99

Connor's Brain
Malcolm Rose

Connor began his second life at the age of fifteen. He started it with a thirty-mile-an-hour brain.

Connor's first life ended when a virus in his brain stripped him of almost everything – his memory, language and a sense of time.

Now Connor lives in a permanent present that he doesn't understand. The 'new' Connor doesn't recognise or remember his parents, his brother, his friends – or his girlfriend Hattie.

New-Connor can't remember the old Connor, but there are people who can. People who have reasons to keep him quiet – or to hurt him.

Because old-Connor had a dark past.

Nominated for the CILIP Carnegie Medal, 2017

ISBN 978-178591-135-4
£7.99

Barbara Catchpole was a teacher for thirty years and enjoyed every minute. She is the author of many books for children and young adults, including the hugely successful (and, she modestly admits, award-winning) PIG and Feely series.

Barbara has three sons of her own who were always perfectly behaved and never gave her a second of worry.

She also tells lies.